Seed Corn

Seed Corn

ANNA BLAIR

SHEPHEARD-WALWYN

Printed and bound in Great Britain
for Shepheard-Walwyn (Publishers) Ltd,
26 Charing Cross Road (Suite 34), London WC2H 0DH
by Cox & Wyman, Reading
from typesetting by Alacrity Phototypesetters,
Banwell Castle, Weston-super-Mare.

British Library Cataloguing in Publication Data

Blair, Anna
  Seed Corn.
  I. Title
  823'.914 [F]

ISBN 0-85683-118-2

Contents

The Dream of
Ishak-Bin-Ibraim

Ishak-bin-Ibraim the Herd, had loved very few things in life since his wife had passed on. Apart from Allah and Muhammad (May Peace and Blessing of Allah be upon Him), of whom he was a faithful disciple, he truly loved only his goats and the roaming of the green Malaysian hillside pastures outside Kuala Lumpur. He had three sons, of course, and when they were spark-eyed and beautiful children he had been a fond and affectionate father and they had been his hopes for the future. But they had long-since grown up and gone their wilful ways. Number One son still went to Friday Prayers but was unfaithful to his wife. Number Two son had married a Thai girl of his own choice and gone away to live in Bangkok, and Number Three son was doomed to Hell for all eternity because he had abandoned the faith of his forefathers and was often heard to take the name of Allah in vain. Ishak saw nothing of his middle son but the other two paid duty visits to him in the one-room thatched hut on the grassy slope above Kampong Sungai (the River Village). These two never came together, for an old quarrel lay between them; and they never brought their children because they lived in neat brick link-houses with fences and gardens round them, and they were ashamed of the atap house where their mother had borne them.

Ishak was a man of middle height, his skin burned dry with constant exposure to the sun. From morning until night he wore a thin baju tunic, and a kain sarong wrapped from waist

1

to ankles round his spare body. His forearms were sinewy and his narrow hands scarred and scratched from a lifetime of rescuing his animals out of thorns and prickly mela-mela thickets. Every morning he wound a faded cotton cloth round his head and let it fall over the back of his grey head to protect it and his wrinkled neck from the sun.

Apart from having obedient and filial offspring and his hardy little wife back from death again to share his sleeping-place, if there had been one other single thing he could have changed about his life it would have been this head-gear. If he, Ishak-bin-Ibraim, could have qualified to wear the white Haji cap instead, then he would have been a whole man in body and spirit and ready to pass on content when his time came. He had no doubt that, if he asked, Number One son could have given him the money to go to Mecca to perform The Haj, if only to appease Allah for having taken the girl Farah for his woman, but that son was a sinful man and his tainted money would have been an insult to Allah and to the memory of the Prophet Muhammad (May Peace and Blessing of Allah be upon Him).

Ishak was a solitary man, but not friendless. The women in the kampong washed his clothes for him and gave him the clean bundle every week when he went down and joined their menfolk for Friday prayers. Sometimes he stayed for an hour or two, ate rice at the kampong stall and listened to the latest gossip. Then he would lift his bundle and climb back up the hill again. During the rest of the week he read the Qu'ran alone and listened for the echo of the muezzin's call to private prayer. His little prayer-mat, worn thin by his knees in exactly the correct places, was the symbol of his absolute devotion to Almighty Allah.

His sons had brought sorrow to his private life, but each day of his working life had lapped quietly against the one before and Ishak had pictured it going on like that until his call came, or until he was struck by some disabling illness ... Please to Allah for a quick end ... There was nothing short of paralysis that he could foresee stopping his early morning rise, and

2

each day's tending of the twenty-three goats in his charge.

Over recent months he had watched the yellow mechanical giants far over to the south of Kampong Sungai, swallowing great gulps of jungle and grassland and spewing it out again, first as fiery red dust and then as row upon row of link-houses like the ones he supposed his sons lived in. He loved the land where he toiled and, as he stretched out his bamboo pole and tapped the rump of Ishak Two, who had a grey pointed beard like his own and Kechil, the little one, or Gemuk the fat, he would shake his head at this savaging of Allah's countryside and turn instead to feast his eyes on the peace of his own pastures. Najib-bin-Idris, his master, might own these acres on paper, but Ishak had never thought of them as any other than his own.

Najib came to see him one day in January as he brought in his goats. They talked of this and that, and then suddenly Ishak could not believe what the farmer was saying. His master, Najib selling his land? ...

"... and so the goats go to the first market after Chinese New Year, Ishak."

Ishak found not a single word to say, but a tic jumped in his leathery cheek that had not been seen since the day they had told him that his Number One son had another woman. He stood now as if he had been stripped naked, and Najib-bin-Idris for his part wished, by the Prophet, that he had found a better way to tell the old man, or that he had not had to tell him at all.

"The developers want the land," he explained, as if to a child. There was still only that stricken stare in the old eyes.

"People ... young people ... need houses. You are old, Ishak, you have worked all your life ... so hard too. Now you can rest."

Then Najib spoke of the ringgit. He had not intended so much money for his herd, but the contractor was paying him richly for his land, and although the old Ishak was making him angry just now, he had been goat-herd to Najib's father and his grand-father before him, and he himself would scarcely have noticed the loss of three times what he proposed to give Ishak to compensate him.

Long after the master had left his goat-herd, the old man was still standing there, scratching at the neck of Kechil and muttering about the frailty of men who had to live in brick and tile houses. Then he saw that the lights were beginning to flicker over in the kampong and heard the evening's first 'choonk' from the nightjar bird. He settled the animals and took the winding path up towards home. It would soon be time to unroll his rug and turn towards Mecca when the call came.

It was during the last line of his prayers that he remembered the money Najib had spoken of. And then the amount of it came to mind. Enough, and a little left over. He sat up late and considered. No goats ... but a Haji cap! Perhaps in this way Allah had chosen for Ishak-bin-Ibraim to make the pilgrimage to Mecca to perform his Haj at last.

He must have told someone in the kampong, although he was usually a reticent man. But this was too big a thing to keep secret. Perhaps he told more than one. Because the day after Gemuk, Kechil and the rest had gone forever, Number Three son (the one who had given up the Faith) came to visit.

Ishak understood only snatches and knew that he should be rejoicing over what he heard.

"I have come back to Allah again, Father. But for the sinful years ... penance ... I go ... the Haj ... Allah would be more merciful. My money tied up, still much to pay for my house ... cannot go to brother Abdul, we quarrel you remember ... but they are saying Najib-bin-Idris gave you a small fortune ... You would never go at your age ..."

Father never spoke once while son was talking. He listened. And temptation tore him apart. A cleverer man than Ishak would not have been able to unscramble right from wrong. But Allah was All-Knowing and Compassionate.

*

With the rest of the money Ishak bought five plastic buckets, ten brooms, packets of nuts and seeds, a box of clothes pegs and five cartons of assorted canned foods. Some of the men helped him to take his old home apart plank by plank, carry it down the hill to the kampong and raise it there as a shop-house.

It was on his seventy-eighth birthday that Ishak sat for the first time behind the rough counter of his store, waiting for customers. In time he became used to his new life, enjoying the stir of the kampong better than he had expected.

When his son came home from Mecca that next November with the coveted title, Haji Hassan-bin-Ishak, he took his father to Tun Perak Street in the town and bought him a black velvet songkok. Every morning after that, before going through to his shop, the old man set it carefully on his head. It was quite precious to him, for it meant a lot of things.

In his heart, though, he still longed for the Haji cap. But who knew ... in a year or two ... perhaps if the shop were to do well ...

The Ambitions
of Joshua Trumbill

By day Joshua Trumbill worked as a delivery cadger for one of the wealthy merchants of Glasgow, and this connection had given him delusions of grandeur as pompous as any of the city's great Tobacco Lords. Indeed, although barely into middle-age, he had the portly figure and the very strut of such a personage and, in the twilight, wearing the threadbare red coat and dated tricorn that he had bought at the Saltmarket rag fair, he thought he might easily have been mistaken for one. Certainly there was something of a strain on the buttons across his ample front, but that was true too, of the real Lords who walked the plainstane-pavings doing business by word of mouth, and chasing off intruders on their holy ground, with a flick of their tall silver-knobbed canes.

It was Joshua's unlikely ambition to *be* somebody someday, a councillor perhaps. If not a bailie! Though even he had doubts about the possibility of that. But he did hold another civic position, the title of which, if said quickly enough, might well have misled a stranger or impressed a simple country girl. 'Bumbailie' was the word. Joshua was a Saturday night bumbailie, and, in fact, he had just such a simple country girl in mind to impress. To this end he applied himself with vigour to the bumbailie-ing, to the apprehending of a good count of wild stravaigers on Saturday evenings, ordering them home to prepare decently with their families for the Sabbath next day. Then he would report his tally of catches punctiliously to Master Wilson the Session Clerk before the morning diet of worship. It was fortuitous for Joshua that the lass he had in mind to honour with his attentions was the servant girl at the Session Clerk's house, young highland Morag Macleod. He felt sure that as one of that sober household she would be well aware of his prowess at catching reprobates, and that when he eventually ran to earth a certain rantin' callant in yellow breeches, who tormented him every Saturday night, she would be lost in admiration.

Joshua, with his small eyes, his Sabbath eve activities and his unpleasant habit of eavesdropping on clash not meant for his ears, was not a general favourite in the town, and it was thought that the most sensible and uncharacteristic thing about him was his fancy for sweet, slim Morag.

In spite of the bumbailie's red coat, it was not for a Tobacco House that he cadged in his daily work, but for a general merchant, a dealer in Norwegian tallow, whose main line of small sales was candles. As there was a constant demand for tallows, Joshua had a steady round of calls ... one of which was to the Clerk's house, where he was able to enjoy regular glimpses of bonnie Miss Morag.

Actually, although he would see her flushed and prettier than ever, bent over the cooking fire or scraping the black broth-pot, it was not the servant girl he dealt with on those visits, but the Widow Skinner, who was housekeeper to the Clerk and his ailing wife. She was a worthy woman in her forties, but she was curmudgeonly and saved her unpractised smiles, not for her fading mistress into whose shoes she nurtured fond hopes of stepping in the fullness of time, but for good Master Wilson himself. The maidservant did not sulk under the housekeeper's tart tongue, for she had no wish to be sent back to the wildness of Skye when she had barely tasted the delights of Glasgow.

Morag was a periwinkle of a girl whose bright blue eyes had an imp in them which did not match Joshua's thought of her as 'simple'. She wore a blue kerchief, washed freshly every Monday with her white bib-apron, when she took the rest of the household duds for their weekly tubbing. Her coarse dark green skirt fell to just the very length to show off, to best advantage, slim ankles and feet that had remained shapely and supple from a young lifetime of going barefoot.

Unfortunately for Joshua Trumbill, Morag had no notion whatsoever of him, not only because she found even the idea of a kiss from him distasteful, but because she had a likely lad of her own, handsome, lively and no more than two years older than herself, who was worth a dozen Joshuas. The bumbailie might call twice a week at Clerk Wilson's house (once with the tallows and once with the clipes) but Morag saw her curly-headed Adam, and heard his cheerful whistle, three or four times a day when she was going between the house and the town Green in the course of her chores. Adam Dunlop was, in fact, Joshua's yellow-breeked bugbear and was one of the town herds. Sometimes he collected the cows in twos and threes from their various owners and led them up the Cow Loan to the common grazing north-west of the Cross, but more often he brought them down towards the riverside and the Green. He liked his cows and his open-air life, he liked the fruit-stealing from the new mansion-house orchards, and the other mischiefs he got up to of an evening with his friends. A particular pleasure on a Saturday night was to run away from Joshua the bumbailie, baiting him as they fled, for sulking like a 'Tontine face'. Best of all he liked to feel the blue eyes of Morag Macleod smiling on him when he handed over her jug, brim-full and warm from the milking, or as he heaved up her wooden stoups when she came to the well by the Green for her morning household water supply. He liked it too when he helped her to gather up her bleaching after it had had a day in the sun on the grass, and they could squeeze hands secretly under the sweet-smelling bundle.

And that was the way of it during a certain warm autumn of the 1750s and on the Saturday morning of one of Joshua's calls at Session Clerk Wilson's back-yard door.

"Your caun'les, Mistress Skinner, ma'am." He leaned his plump shoulder against the door-frame and his small eyes devoured Morag greedily as she scrubbed the flagstone floor and blew tendrils of fair hair away from her eyes. She felt his gaze and turned her back.

"Now mind, you'll need to bring mair caun'les now the longer nights is comin' in, Joshua Trumbill," the Widow was saying as she examined the candles for short lengths or wasteful bends, while Joshua put a fat hand on Morag's neat rump. The girl turned a stormy face on him then clattered her bucket across the flags to scrub in a far corner.

In spite of that, Joshua went away quite cheered, unaware of anything between Morag and Adam Dunlop, and preening himself that he had detected a come-hither glance in the girl's eyes as her creamy arm had made furious sweeping circles with the sudsy scrubbing brush. He trundled up the High Street, a silly smile on his round face, muttering and plotting to himself how best to win into her heart, for was not his tally of reportings to the session now close to a hundred?

"Aye, I'll get that Yellow Breeks one o' they Sat'day nights. I'd like fine to make him my roun' hundredth, for he's naethin' but an ill-bent scally, and gude folk'll be glad to see him up afore the session."

Among the gude folk he surely placed the innocent lassie from Skye and, alongside that assurance, was certain that men had risen to be councillors on lesser feats.

The sound of the Tron steeple bells, which marked the time of morning for the merchant men of the city to fill the taverns, drink their ale and pursue their deals, was also the signal for Morag to take the second trip of the day to the well.

"Mind and dinnae loiter there. You've your work waitin' here wi' that fowl the master's to hae to his supper . . . and the mistress o' course," warned the Widow. "I ken how you lassies gets tagled wi' silly clash at that well." And so she did, for was that not how, twenty years before, she had caught the late Sol Skinner?

"Och, an' you know I would never be doing any such a thing, Mistress Skinner. But there's nony a drop of water in that stoup." And Morag fixed her hair braid, whisked off her thibbet apron, tied on a fresh white one and hummed happily to herself as she skipped down the Saltmarket with her stoups.

Morag loved the town. It was pleasant at this hour when the weather was fine and there was no mire to stick to the feet. There was horse dung but that was easily skirted. Born and reared on a silent windswept island, the girl found the city brave and exciting. There was the bellman now, crying that there was a small arrival of meat, and the housewives with the quickest pattens racing to reach the fleshers' barrows for first choice. There was the colour and laughter of the fine dandy merchants spilling out of the taverns back to work, and there were boys coming up the street from the Broomielaw, dangling strings of silver herrings.

Now she had reached the Green and was at the well queue. She took up her position, turned one stoup upside-down and sat on it, moving place by place to the head of the line. There were other island girls there and they teased the rest by whispering their secrets in the Gaelic. Further over she could see Adam laughing with two other herds, and called to him. He came over and sat for a few minutes on her other bucket, telling her that one of the bigger cattle-owners, pleased with his work, had offered him a cow of his own in return for some extra hours' labour. They talked of his morning and hers and exchanged the day's clash.

"That Joshua Trumbill was lookin' on me very bold again today, Adam. He is as old as my father and he dared to put his hand on me." She was the more indignant when she thought on the spare, worthy figure of that Skye crofter, who treated his worn-handed wife as if she was the greatest lady on earth. "My father would not insult my mother so ... and they are wed!"

Adam was a good-natured boy and up till now his tormenting of the bumbailie had not been malicious, but the thought of that candle-greasy paw laid on any part of his Morag incensed him.

Widow Skinner did have cause to scold her kitchen girl after all that noon, for she and Adam had taken two turns round the Green, the water slopping on their feet as they made plans that boded ill for the hapless Joshua. A refill of the stoups, a quick kiss and they parted with a giggling promise to meet again later.

Glasgow should have slept the sounder in those years for its Night Watchmen patrolling their beats in every street, and crying the hours and half hours. But there was another little ritual that often defeated the purpose of the Watch. On the hour each Watch was required to make for the end of the street which was his own beat, step out beyond its junction with the main Trongate, and stand there holding up his lantern, thus reporting in for inspection, part of a lighted rank in which gaps could easily be spotted. But this left the other end of the streets dark, unwatched and clear for various felonies and break-ins, and also for the young, who found their homes too staid for them on Saturday nights, to snatch the safe ten minutes of the hourly lamp-drill to enjoy a bit of horse-play or canoodling undisturbed.

But this was also the happy-hunting time and ground for the bumbailie, and Joshua had been assuring himself all day that, tonight, when the lamps lined up at the low end of the side streets, he would be up round the top end to catch that limb-of-Satan in the yellow breeches, march him in person to Master Session Clerk's house where he had no doubt of seeing Morag ready for household prayers, and wide-eyed at his success.

Widow Skinner had made a call that evening, where incidentally she had heard a disturbing rumour that the Session Clerk was as good as promised to the daughter of a fellow tea-merchant as soon as the dwyning Mistress Wilson had gone to her reward. When Morag had been escorting the housekeeper back from her visit, the streets were full of the clap of pattens and the bobbing, flickering lanterns of other maidservants on the same errand with their mistresses, for all good people had to be gathered safely in for their Sabbath preparations. Morag saw the Widow in, and her back turned to the swee to stir tomorrow's broth, then slipped out again to meet Adam. On the streets by that time of night there were only the last of the godly turning into closes and yard gates and the villains who were cocking a snook at propriety and preparing to outsmart the Night Watch and the Kirk Seizers. The last thing she heard as she crossed the yard was Mistress Skinner's sharp reminder.

"Ten minutes, my lass, mind. No more nor that. You be back here in good time for the Readin'."

Morag and the Widow had played out this scene for a number of Saturday nights now, the housekeeper not actually 'seeing' her go, but happy enough to have the master to herself for their last sup when his wife had retired for the night. This evening she hoped to detect from the way he spoke with her whether the clash about the other tea-merchant's daughter was true. So long as Morag appeared in the house in time for evening devotions she turned a blind eye to the short excursion. The maid was a sensible enough lassie and couldn't come to much harm with the herd in ten minutes. There was a queer core in Mistress Skinner that was not entirely cold. It was deep-set ... but it was there.

Usually Joshua Trumbill had a fair hunt of the wynds and alleys before he caught sight of Adam Dunlop and then it was usually fleeting and in vain, but tonight he had scarcely started on his way up the High Street when he saw the kenspeckle Yellow Breeches whisking into Greyfriars Wynd ... *and* he had a lassie with him ... double villainy! Joshua puffed up and down and along after them and saw the reckless pair halfway down the Candleriggs before they disappeared into a vennel. Joshua smirked. There was only one way they could go now. It was in the Back Cow Loan that the bumbailie came on them, brazenly kissing, and there that he finally achieved his ambition. He took the herd into custody by grasping his wrists from the back and pinioning them behind him, against his shoulder blades.

"Your sort's a' talk" he sneered, holding Adam in one hand now and grasping the girl by her elbow, then frogmarching them towards the High Street. Joshua swelled with pride as they approached Master Wilson's house. It had all been surprisingly easy and he wished he could have seen their faces in the dark, at this come-uppance.

"Them as behaves theirsel's indecent and doesnae get ready for the Sabbath aye gets what deserves them richt," he said piously, tightening his grip. Suddenly the herd twisted out of his grasp.

"So does them as bullies and clipes ..." And somehow Joshua was spreadeagled on his back with, for guidsakes, the lassie astride his chest! Only, by the light from a one-up window chink he could see it wasnae a lassie at a', it was that fell villain, the herd, and, what was worse, Yellow Breeks, that was standing laughing at him ... was laughing from the face of his sweet Morag Macleod, and pulling out the skirt she had had bundled up round her waist. His spirit groaned.

"Now listen you here Bumbailie Trumbill," Adam was saying. "You ken this is the Sabbath eve and you've had your arms round this lassie a' the way fae the Back Cow Loan, molesting her, for she didnae want you. You wouldnae like that bruited round the toon. So, when we get the length of Mistress Skinner's kitchen, you just haud your wheesht. Mind that and gie's your word, or we'll hae to set here a' nicht."

All credit to Joshua, it took two or three bounces of the skinny herd's sharp haunches on his chest before he gave in. Then Adam stood aside, wheeched off Morag's old scrubbing skirt from his waist and dragged the winded bumbailie to his feet.

The housekeeper was gloomily setting her kitchen to rights for the morrow, misery in every line of her for the certainty she had now that she would never be the second Mistress Wilson, when the three opened the door and stood just outside. When Morag was excited the soft ss-es of her west highland speech sang like the sea; a shutter across the street was opened a crack and an eye peered out.

"D'you know this, Mistress Skinner ..." Morag was saying, "Maister Trumbill here has been telling us what a grand fancy he has for you, but so shy he is to call on you with his respec's ..." Then Adam chimed in "... that we've brung him wirsel's to make his first visit ..."

The shutter across the way opened wider, and hastily

Mistress Skinner ushered Joshua into the kitchen. Morag followed demurely while Adam melted into the darkness. Lost for a moment for words the housekeeper poured Joshua a serving of the Session Clerk's best wine (which she poured the more generously for her pique at the master). There were only ten minutes before the Book would be on the good room table upstairs and the Clerk looking at his clock, but it was enough to restore and re-channel the Widow's hopes. She was a daunting woman and when Joshua saw the shutter opposite still agape as he left the kitchen to wander dazedly along the High Street he knew, not only that Morag was not for him, but that he was hopelessly compromised with the Widow.

Behind him, upstairs now, through every word of the chapter from Isaiah, Mistress Skinner was sinfully taking stock. Joshua Trumbill, she supposed, for all his faults, was a worthy man, steady of character and not so ill and puny to look on as her first man. She might make something of him yet. And so in those few mischievous words of Morag's about his 'grand fancy' the bumbailie's fate of taking on Master Skinner's purposeful relict was as good as sealed.

As for Adam, who was still carrying Morag's skirt under his oxter as he went whistling down towards the Tolbooth, he was pleased with the night's work, surely the crown of all his callant shennanigans with Joshua and others of his kind. But he was thinking too that maybe he was getting to be too much of a man for such capers, that Morag was already woman enough, and that it was high time they were wed and staying at home, douce and domestic, of a Sabbath eve. He would take on the extra work and the cow of his own and by-and-by they would be passing rich and well content.

Their wedding banns were cried for the first time two weeks later; funny enough, on the same day as those of Joshua Trumbill with the Widow Skinner's.

In the end Morag and Adam grew rounder as they grew older, with good food, happiness and family life: while Joshua, at the neb end of Mistress Trumbill's tongue, grew thinner and thinner until the red coat in which he had fancied he looked

14

like a Tobacco Lord, drooped on him, the good leg he'd flashed in his prime was but a shank and his too-big buckled shoes skliffed on the cobbles.

But he did eventually become a councillor. Mistress Trumbill saw to that.

The Day Gran'maw Spoke

The old woman had been sitting her days out speechless on the Steillmans' porch as long as some of their neighbours could remember ... at least the newer-comers. There were still those who could recall her as a brisk New England matron, jangling with chunky jewellery, with a blue rinse through her hair and going faithfully to three different monthly luncheon clubs. There were even fewer who remembered the days when she sang in the Bethany Church choir. Now her only connection with the Bethany was that the new young pastor prayed, from time to time, for strength for Marti and Ed to carry the burden of care they had 'ever with them'. But most of her contemporaries had passed on, others were housebound or gazing into emptiness in the concrete-paved gardens of Sunset Homes where no weeds grew and there was no perfume from the flowers.

Marti and Ed Steillman lived in a white shingle house they called "River Green" on a two-acre spread of grassland a mile or two inland from Long Island Sound. There were willow trees, maples and a few firs there, and a narrow quiet-flowing river marking their boundary. Beyond that lived their own daughter and her family, noisy, affectionate and as much at home on the Steillmans' place as at their own. Their other three were within an hour's ride and, as Marti said, at least once a week to Ed, "Guess we're blest, Ed-fellow, that's what." Nevertheless she appreciated the pastor's prayers because it seemed like forever that she'd had her Mom sitting on that porch.

It was eight years since the old woman had had a slight stroke. After that she'd fumbled with her food a little, but the doctors were puzzled that, over the years since the incident, she seemed to have lost the power of speech too, and even the will to fight. It wasn't even that she was deaf, they said. Marti wasn't so sure of that. But whatever it was, the Steillmans had concluded long ago that what they had on their hands was but the husk of a woman, vegetating in her rocker on their back porch, lost in some far world of her own that they couldn't reach. Now they didn't even try.

Sometimes Marti thought dementedly that the steady creak of that rocker would be the end of her . . . back and forth, back and forth, with a kind of rasp every few seconds where the curve of the rocker hit a knot on the porch floor. But, most of the time, like the rest, she almost forgot her mother altogether. Or at least that she'd ever been a person at all. No words passed between them now, nor even an affectionate pressure of their hands. She was just something to be got up, washed, diapered, sat in the rocker and served with food and drink three times a day; and between spring and fall, taken in only at night or if torrential rain battered its way into the porch. And not always until one of Ed and Marti's grandchildren would remember, and turn from staring out at the sodden ground.

"What about Gran'maw?" And Gran'maw would be led mechanically inside to the back room, where no one else sat, steered to the rattan chair plum in front of a small T.V. Whoever had brought her in would flick the switch and they would all have the illusion that the old woman was being entertained. The family was pre-occupied rather than unkind. Ed was a peaceable, easy-going big man, who had surprised his more dynamic contemporaries by getting ahead in his oil-related construction business without working nights or having an analyst, making as much money as they did in theirs without laying up the coronaries they suffered by pushing themselves too hard and forgetting to take vacations. So there were not even outbursts or tensions to draw attention to the old woman at all, as an issue between Ed and Marti. They had been married for nearly forty years . . . so long that it was only friends who noticed that the worst Ed ever did was to sigh and say "Aw Honey . . ." when Marti thrust her mother's tray at him the minute he was home and before he'd even opened the 'fridge for a can of beer. And by the time he'd reach the porch he'd have forgotten even that mild explosion and absently deliver the tray without a word.

There was no point in speaking, for the old woman had forgotten everything. She'd lived a long time and there was a lot to forget . . . the sixty years in New England that Ed and Marti knew something about, and twenty-three before that in the Old Country that were way back beyond time to them . . . the years before the old woman and her Willie had come out as a young couple to be new Americans, bringing only their modest savings and the infant in their arms with the name she'd been given for her Scottish grandmother, Martha Baillie. Marti had never been interested in her roots and the years of her mother's youth were a closed book to her.

Ed Steillman was a laconic man. The answers 'Yep', 'Nope' and 'Some', in the relevant places were his idea of social conversation and the jargon of his trade all that was required in business. All the same he was hospitable and that Sunday he had invited to supper an overseas expert in computing who was casting his eye over the Steillman Inc. accounts system to see how it could be streamlined.

Ed's directions to the man to find the house had been vague and Alec Raeburn had set out too soon so that, hot and uncomfortable and conscious of being inopportune, he arrived at "River Green" a little early. Ed was still shopping for steaks and sauces at the mall supermarket three miles away. Marti saw their visitor at the side gate in the white fence and came out, flustered herself, but with the smile of the determined American hostess on her face and "Welcome" in every line of her figure, still svelte in the cherry pants-suit she'd hoped to change before he came.

"Alec isn't it? I'm Marti. Ed's not home right now, but he'll be along. Come in the house and have a cold drink."

As Raeburn put his foot on to the porch step a telephone bell rang inside. Marti held up a helpless hand.

"Take a seat. I gotta see who's calling." She bustled away and Alec mounted the few steps.

What with the bell, their footfall on the bare wood floor and their greetings, he was seated and stretching out his legs before he heard the creak of the rocker in the shadows at the back of the porch, and saw the old woman in the faded blue cotton dress. He was a polite man and got to his feet immediately, bowed slightly and held out his hand.

"Pardon me, ma'am ... I'm sorry I didn't catch your name from Mrs. Steillman ... and I didn't see you sitting so quietly there."

The rasp of the rocker came monotonous and regular as a metronome. The parchment face did not alter. Her lower teeth had been broken two years now, and they hadn't thought it worthwhile to get her new ones and so her jaws had sunk, settling themselves into her gums. Her washed-out eyes stared across the grass. Raeburn's hand dropped. He bowed awkwardly again and sat down.

"Fine yard you got here ... and the bushes back there on the sidewalk ..." he groped for a word ... "they're 'neat'." He was humouring her as he might have tried to cajole a child by using its own slang. Maybe these were the right words, maybe not. It didn't matter anyhow. There was no response. He tried a few more pleasantries, but she took no notice. If it hadn't been for the swing of the chair he might even have thought to touch and see if she hadn't perhaps died since the family had last looked.

Alec Raeburn was an owlish young man with no other remarkable physical features than wide open eyes behind round spectacles. His hair was medium brown, height medium tall, build medium sturdy and his skin had the uneasy red-brown of a new tan. But he was as absorbent as lint, to information and fresh experience, curious about everything. He resented time spent in unfamiliar territory without his questions about it being satisfied. He was usually irked by silence in those circumstances, but it was humid today, in the high nineties on the computer displays outside banks and offices, so it was restful to turn his attention to what there was worth observing across the meadow land in front of the porch as it sloped down to the river. Now he could hear children playing and arguing. A breath of wind that seemed more like a sigh of heat turned the lazy leaves of the weeping willow. He glimpsed a flash of cream and black that he knew was a chipmunk scrabbling at the base of an old oak tree. In an ancient maple a grey squirrel was louping nervously towards a drey in the topmost branches, pausing and twitching as the shouts of the children from over the fence bounding the neighbour's land, echoed across the grass, one voice whining and whimpering above the rest. Through the trees he saw a small girl sulking and leaning against a basketball post.

Suddenly Raeburn was startled to see a second squirrel running, swift and sure as a zip fastener, along a telephone cable. He exclaimed and turned instinctively to point it out to the old woman. But still she sat there like a swaying image. He had not shared his moment and when he looked again the squirrel was gone.

A scattering of red-breasted thrush-birds he knew were American robins attracted him next, and he caught his lip in annoyance when the petulant wailing of the child next-door rose to a yell and the birds flew off.

"My! But she's a bad-tempered wee lassie that ... ettlin' for a right good spankin'," he said to no one but the empty acres and his own irritated self.

The wailing stopped as if the child had heard his threat. And then he was aware that the rocking chair had broken rhythm and ceased its creaking.

"Aye," said the old woman distinctly. "It's that wee yin wi' the fernietickles on her nose. She's aye girnin'." There was a pause, but Alec Raeburn supposed that she'd been sleeping, open-eyed somehow, earlier, and was awake now ready to chat with him.

"You're a Scot originally then?" he asked.

"Glasgow."

She was vague in her replies to questions about the chipmunk, and the squirrel on the cable ... so he shrugged mentally and talked instead of his home in Grangemouth and the aunt he used to visit in Springburn as a boy, and in the time it took another squirrel to frisk to the top of the maple, answered a dozen questions from the old woman on Sauchiehall Street, and the old shops and tearooms of the city.

Inside the house Marti heard the voices on the porch and sent Ed, who had just come in from the garage with the youngest grandchild, to see what other visitor they had and what they would all have to drink. Ed stopped short at the porch door, stunned to hear Gran'maw carrying on a conversation with this total stranger. The youngest grandchild, who had never heard her speak before, ran away crying. Ed backed into the shade of the house again to fetch his wife.

Marti reached the porch in time to hear her mother argue with their visitor that Glasgow was a finer city than Edinburgh, and stepped forward rubbing nervous hands on the cherry pants-suit.

"Gran'maw ..." she began.

"It's you, Martha. This is my daughter Martha." Marti just stood. Her mother scolded.

"Martha, Mr. Raeburn here's come a' the way fae Grangemouth ... he'll be needin' his tea."

Alec Raeburn enjoyed the Steillmans' company until quite late and had all his questions answered about racoons and chipmunks, the height of the Empire State and the follies of the present administration. Only once did the old woman speak again that day, to tell him that her man, Willie, had been a plumber in Glasgow when they met. But that was while Ed and Marti were in the kitchen stacking dirty dishes in the washer.

Ed drove Alec back to his hotel and by the next weekend Raeburn had flown home.

It was too late now for Marti and Ed to learn the only

21

language the old woman remembered. By Monday her chair had taken up its endless rocking again and she was silent. By the following Sunday they wondered if they had been dreaming, and by Thanksgiving only the youngest grandchild remembered that Gran'maw had spoken that summer.

The Barbarian

There were few of her matron friends back in Rome who envied Claudia her husband's posting to the Empire's wild north-west frontier. Gaul, or the Rhine, even South Britain where people had begun to take on Roman ways, would have been bearable, thinkable. But not the bleak Caledonian mists or the savage natives that lurked behind them.

They did agree though that, of all of them, the purposeful Claudia, daughter of a proud patrician family, was the one who could best endure such a fate. Strong, determined and tall as her husband, Marcus Valerian the legion commander, she was the one who could make a home as nearly befitting a Roman family as the wilderness and distance from civilisation would allow.

In fact Claudia was well able to order her days very nearly as she might have done at home. Although the first wooden forts behind the narrow ditches and earth ramparts had been replaced by stone buildings, double ditches and more compacted barriers, those were still the early days after the legion's push northward, and the great wall that the Emperor Hadrian would raise was still half-a-century in the future.

But even in Claudia's time the settlements themselves were engineered and orderly with broad principal streets, barracks and store-houses, homes, stables and baths. And although there was less of the usual social intercourse among officer families than in most small towns of the Empire, nevertheless there was always the pleasure of making short journeys between forts to spend hours with other friends stationed there.

Claudia prided herself on being self-sufficient and able to fill up her days with the running of the household. She organised her slaves to see to the thrifty garnering of grain in the cellars and the shovelling of wood and charcoal into the hypocaust stoves for the heating ducts. She supervised the wise storage in sturdy amphorae of the precious fine wines, carried to them from their home vineyards, station by station, along great roads. There was the caring for family linen too, and ornaments, for they were not easily replaced. Almost most vital of all, there was the study of herbs and salves for healing the gripes and fevers of an alien climate, and the conserving of perfumed oils to anoint the body after bathing.

But higher on Claudia's heart than any of those matters was the proper raising of her only daughter, Lucia, to fill her destined position after these days of exile, as a Roman wife and mother, back home in the heart of the Empire itself. Many of the advantages Lucia should have enjoyed were not available to her anywhere along the road linking the chain of forts and stations, and even fewer when the weather confined the girl to their own quarters. The quality of music-making, games and drama was limited by whatever talents were thrown up among soldiers and artisans and their families there. The few other young women available for company were not precisely the companions Claudia would have chosen for her daughter, not being of comparable rank, and there was a grave shortage of young male escorts of the type who would have frequented their villa in Rome in gratifying numbers, as suitors with impeccable qualifications.

But what was humanly possible Claudia did for Lucia. The girl was her mother's right hand at all the housewifely arts which were not those more properly the work of slaves ... fine stitching, the garnishing of meals, the arranging of table and glasses, the overseeing of servants. She taught her to sing and to accompany herself on the small harp. They read together from the Greek and Latin poets, and an hour, morning and evening, was spent walking up and down the length of the villa courtyard to acquire the gliding deportment and elegant postures she would need if she was not to be an object of mirth or pity when their posting in the wilds was over. They even danced with invisible partners until Claudia was satisfied that, when the time came, Lucia could take her place among real partners at any celebration without gaucherie or embarrassment. Nor were the changing fashions of the rest of the Empire ignored. Newcomers and visitors brought the newest hair-combs, wristlets and necklaces for the commander's family, and word of the current cut and hang of dresses. New-minted coins were examined for the latest arrangement of the hair. 'When the time comes' was the great incentive for all the rigours of learning, polishing and keeping-up, that Lucia underwent.

So the three or four years in the far north was but a marking-time for fulfilment, and by her fifteenth birthday Lucia was a well-groomed virgin of Rome with a firm belief in the divine right of her countrymen to be wherever in the world they cared to plant the eagle, and in the absolute conviction that the Caledonians to the north of rampart and ditch were ferocious and untamed, forever snapping like wild dogs at the heels of Rome.

Any coming and going between forts, of women or other civilians, was strictly on the south side of the line where local people had grown used to occupation and pursued their lives much as they had always done, but modified by the nearness of the Roman presence and the advantages it brought to them. But fort civilians went nowhere on that south side unescorted, and nowhere at all to the dangerous north.

What went on there was known to Lucia only by hearsay and the constant reference to its natives as Caledonian 'savages'.

Claudia could not help but feel gratified at the sight of her proud, tall daughter with her dark hair piled in high ringlets on a shapely head, and at the sound of her well-modulated voice as she talked and moved easily among the other fort people, kindly enough, but never tempting them to forget their position by condescending from her position as Marcus Valerian's daughter.

If Claudia sighed from time to time it was only that such a paragon, in the first glory of womanhood, was not seen to advantage among the patrician families in the sunshine of home, where there would surely be a high-born mate worthy of her daughter. There still remained more than a year of their posting here. What Claudia feared most was that the winds and rain off the surrounding hills would weather that fine bloom off Lucia's cheeks before she could be presented in the marriage market in Rome.

Marcus Valerian himself, in spite of his pre-occupation with administration, building and the constant surveillance of the fierce land to the north, was a fond father, as well aware as his wife that Lucia's chances of a good match could be passing her by. And so it was with satisfaction that he returned home from a visit to the fort at Vindolanda with news for his wife and daughter. He found them in the small ante-room of the bath-house resting with their needlework in the warm air rising from the hypocaust, and safe from chill outside, while a slave girl gently massaged Lucia's slim white feet. Marcus slipped off his cloak, and raised his hand to have wine brought.

"Lydia sends her greetings from Vindolanda, Claudia, but scolds me for not having taken you on my visit. Next time I'm not to dare appear alone."

"She's well ... and Paulinus and the children?"

"Paulinus is as hardy as ever, the others have blains on their hands from the frost, but the young ones are as noisy and lively as ever." Marcus paused to convey that he had real news of his journey away, "... *and* ... they have a visitor from Rome."

Claudia caught his tone, and after a moment Lucia caught her mother's.

"A visitor?"

"The Tribune Quintus Silvanus. He's been at Camulodonum and is to be at Vindolanda for some months, before going back to Rome."

Quintus Silvanus was the son of the Senator Silvanus and Claudia's friend Julia. That was his first recommendation. But he was also related to the Emperor — he was wealthy, clever and ambitious for advancement, and when they were last in Rome he had been the young lion of the moment, warmly lauded, talked of among those who mattered, as a coming man. Meanwhile he was serving his Emperor and widening his experience, laying careful foundation for future preferment in Rome, the very hub of civilisation. He was all that a far-seeing mother could have wanted for her daughter, and Claudia, who had schooled and trained her filly for just such a match, had instantly half-a-dozen plans and projects towards bringing it about.

"Quintus must find his first weeks lonely, so far north," she said, folding up her needlework. Marcus observed mildly that the young man's stay would be short and that anyway he would have the company of several hundred others at Vindolanda.

"But not others of his own class," Claudia was sure, and pitied her husband's stupidity. He placated her.

"I thought the tribune would do well to visit other forts besides Vindolanda. He's to spend some time here with us when he can be spared, and then go further west to see the stations there." Valerian was not blind to his own prospects, with his family linked to the Emperor's.

Lucia knew perfectly well what was afoot and her natural excitement was tempered slightly by her own recollection of Quintus Silvanus as a rather heavy-faced young man she had once seen throwing aside a frightened slave and kicking him for some trifling misdemeanor. But perhaps the servant had been guilty of more than one fault and Quintus had finally lost patience. He was certainly handsome and she had known, even as a small girl, that whoever married him would live in luxury and sunshine for the rest of her life . . . that there would be no more enduring cold winds and cutting rain at the edge of the world. She would have to be patient until he came.

Lucia had seen three winters come and go at the fort and two summers that had been only a little less bleak, . . . sodden, sunless and leaden of sky; and she thought the days here must be everlastingly grey, whatever the season. And so it was with a shock of surprised delight in this third springtime that she saw the dun-coloured hills bathed in clear, sharp sunlight. Then April came, the air grew warmer and, when she slipped up to stand beside one of the soldiers at a rampart look-out towards the north, she saw that the land was fresh and green with burns sparkling and splashing down over rocky outcrops. The grass was bright, starred with wild flowers, and tan and green lustred birds darted about among the mounds and tussocks.

The south side of the fort was always busy and noisy with the coming and going of men and animals and Lucia knew it well. It was the assembly area for setting out and the dispersal point at home-comings. The ground was beaten bare where it was not yet surfaced, and it was not a place to wander and enjoy. But for the first time, now that she had glimpsed the forbidden territory to the north, Lucia felt the urge to roam a little there among those flowers and burns and the fresh green of the grass. She did hesitate, for that was where the wild Caledonians lived in the strange, round hovels her parents talked about. But they were out of sight and she would not stray too far into danger. She would keep well within sight of the fort.

There was no great difficulty about getting there. There were ways over and through ramparts for essential coming and going by legionaries and messengers. Implicit obedience to the code for military families had always been barrier enough. But Lucia, perhaps bored, and impatient for Quintus Silvanus to come, was set on breaking the rules. Her mother was resting, the fort was about its business and a quick whisk of her cloak past the back of a careless soldier, and Lucia was out, almost at once into the concealing fold of a low hill beside a chattering burn not visible to the sentry.

She walked cautiously alongside the stream, feeling the cool grass damp against her ankles, and delighted by the sight of a yellow furred tree leaning over the water and the dark blue flowers that nestled underneath. Reeds and yellow-cups grew there in great clumps and, when she knelt to pick some, she startled a pair of grey and yellow birds flitting in and out along the overhanging branch.

Was this the wild land where civilised people could disappear for ever, cannibalised by men who lived like animals, underground ... this enchanted place? Perhaps that was it. Perhaps she was bewitched. If she was, she did not care and was drawn on, winding with the burn, past foxgloves and blackthorn and creamy eddying pools.

And then she saw one of them. At the water's edge. One of the barbarians, the merciless men who defied the soldiers of Rome themselves. Lucia stood stockstill behind a bush, helpless even to turn and run. He had not seen her. Perhaps when the blood flowed back into her legs she could slip away again to the safety of the fort.

She watched him. He was kneeling with his arms round a young goat. She could see the sun shining on his reddish-fair hair and that he was not much older than she was herself. Then she saw that the kid's forelegs were caught between two stones in the burn and that the boy was trying to free them. The animal bleated pitifully and the savage stroked its head and spoke soothingly. Then he struggled again to shift the stones and Lucia saw blood on the goat's leg. In spite of every instilled law of obedience and common-sense she moved forward, and this time the fright was in the grey eyes of the boy when he looked up and saw her there.

Without speaking Lucia knelt beside him and as he used both hands to push apart the stones, she eased out the bruised and bleeding legs. Then she drew back as he gathered the quivering goat into his arms and rubbed his own cheek softly against its head.

"Thank you ... lost her from others ... came back." He spoke enough stumbling words of her own tongue to make her understand and, for Lucia, after having seen how he gentled and calmed the animal, his words were the second surprise. She would have expected no more than grunts or snarling sounds from a Caledonian Briton.

She knew, then, that he must be one of those who came occasionally bartering their hides and grain, and sometimes meat, for what was available at the fort of poorer wines and salt, or old tools. The fort was cautious of that kind of trade for it happened often enough that a herd or pedlar, with a sharp eye for the lay-out of parts of the fort, had been followed by a horde of fighting men to harass or raid its stores.

The boy bent down to bathe the goat's knees. His hands were strong and square and the sun glinted on golden hairs on his forearms. Lucia knelt beside him to scoop up water over the cuts and grazings. She felt the boy's eyes on her and turned to look at his face. The eyes were clear and grey as if from looking out over long reaches of moorland and sky, and not simply at the kind of clutter of possessions that, even in this forsaken border land, furnished her parents' lives. On his upper lip lay the first shadow of the moustache that would one day grow long and curling, and strike terror into faint-hearted legionaries. He smiled now and the eyes were warm.

Suddenly Lucia took fright at the whole escapade. She turned and ran to where she could watch for the chance to slip back unnoticed to the fort.

She told herself that it was to see that the little goat had recovered, that she went out the next day, across the soft grass and among misty blue flowers down to the hollow of the burn. And the boy told himself that the sweetest grazing for his animals was there, where it was watered by the stream . . . and so without surprise they came on each other again.

The days lengthened into May, the goat was as frisky as her sisters again, the grass by the hollow nibbled short. But still Lucia and the boy met. He pointed out orange-tipped butterflies to her, that she could scarcely see when they folded their wings against the leaves of grey-green thistles. He showed her molehills and brown-headed seabirds, and miller's-thumbs darting in and out of the butterburrs growing purple in the shallows. And he caught a fluttering bird by letting it run headlong into a burrow he had made in the earth. He held it a moment in his hands so that they could see its throbbing feathers, then he lifted it up and gently let it fly free.

There were only a few days that spring and early summer that Lucia and the boy did not meet. Those were the days that

Quintus Silvanus spent on a first fleeting visit to the fort and they were the longest of Lucia's life. Quintus saw the beautiful Lucia, with the added flush she had about her from her love for the herd, and flattered himself that he, the darling of Rome, had put it there. He strolled with her, talking, and boasting of his exploits and his ambitions for the future. Then on the last evening he intimated that when he returned to report to the Emperor he wished it to be with Lucia as his wife. Meantime he had to travel to posts further west, but he would be back shortly to make marriage arrangements with her family.

Claudia wept privately for joy, the good Valerian, seeing all their prospects suddenly fair, gave willing consent and the fort community rejoiced that the commander's daughter had charmed so notable a man (though most were careful to keep out of his way, not to fall foul of him). Lucia herself was stricken. And it was not only because she had been right about Quintus in her childhood days, that he was cruel and vicious. He had an arrogant contempt for slaves and raw soldiers and strutted the station like a god.

As soon as Silvanus was gone to the west and arrangements for the marriage were in hand, she fled the fort and ran to the cover of the low hills beyond the north rampart to find the herd.

It wasn't the first time they had lain together in the soft grass with the burn running by, but it was the one Lucia remembered for ever. He was tender and patient and his touch was gentle. Above them birds wheeled and sang, and she felt her spirit rise exulting with them.

Two weeks they had together, meeting every day, before she watched him lift his hand in a last wave and disappear into a summer heat haze to the north. Then a subdued Lucia pledged herself to the darkly-handsome Silvanus who had returned to claim his bride.

As they left the fort for Vindolanda where they were to pass two months before they would return to Rome, she could hear the celebrations still echoing behind them. Lucia was too young yet to know that the luxury and position she would enjoy in the capital would be some sort of compensation for lost joy, and by the time they reached Rome a disgruntled Quintus was already thinking of more lusty young women he would find there who would have the spirit and response his gloomy young bride so miserably lacked.

But Lucia had the secret of another compensation carried under her heart as they entered Rome and civilisation.

In the spring she gave birth to her child ... a boy with a downy cap of fair golden hair. It was true that one of his feet was slightly turned in, but he was beautiful and Lucia held him close. Quintus was angry that she had given him a son who was deformed. He sulked in the bath-house for two days, but then, impatient for a perfect one and not willing to waste any time, he came and took her again with agonising brutality.

In spite of her pain Lucia rejoiced in this first child, even in the slight lameness that would always halt him a little; for Quintus the sturdy, would despise him for his weakness, neglect him. She was young, there would be other children, children who would be true sons and daughters of the Empire. But this boy would be hers, to wander with her among the hills of Rome, to watch the creatures there, and the flourish of springtime ... hers to love and teach, and rear to be a gentle savage like his father.

The Sewing-Bee

Her fortnightly sewing-bee was the highlight of Nell Minto's life. It was, in fact, almost the only social intercourse she had, independently of the married sister whose home she shared and where she was at the beck and whim of an untidy and thoughtless family of six. She shared that home because she had been asthmatic since childhood, was considered to be too delicate to go out to work, and so had only the slenderest of incomes. In return for her keep and a certain absentminded and spasmodic affection, she tried to run their home. That was so far as it was possible to fight the chaos of irregularly required meals, sodden and strewn bathrooms, the endless succession of surprise overnight guests, litters of books and of the artistic endeavours of painter, potter, and the young weaver who kept her loom in the sunporch. And there was Nell's brother-in-law who daily tramped large clods of his beloved garden into her kitchen. It was a happy, noisy, bohemian household, and it repelled the fastidious Nell to the depth of her soul.

Actually it had been her soul which had put her in touch with the other three in the 'bee' for she had met them through the local church a year or two before. They were kindly women who had observed her shy loneliness and taken her under their collective wing.

Tonight was the first meeting of the autumn and Nell had looked forward to it with an eagerness her friends, with their other interests and pleasures, would barely have understood.

The four women lived in varying sizes and styles of house on a newish suburban housing estate, set round the church, the school and a row of shops.

Tonight it was Joan's bee. The fire was bright and the room arranged for the four, a small table at each elbow, tea-trolley set with best china and silver teapot, one armchair drawn over a worn patch in the carpet and a small damp area on one wall hidden by a parlour-palm. Joan enjoyed their meetings least, when they were at her house. So much was needing to be repaired or replaced if her home was to be upsides with Phyllis's, where everything was modern and tastefully expensive ... or Kate's, which glowed with mahogany and antique silver and where, if the carpet was worn, it was because it came from an auction-room and was a hundred-year-old Persian.

It was all Jack's fault of course. He should have been a headmaster or at least a department principal long ago ...

Greetings were over, hands stretched out to the fire, and they were on to enquiries about families while they rummaged to take out knitting and sewing. Someone asked for Jack. Joan, sitting on the edge of her chair in a dress that was nearly a year old, and twisting her wedding ring with thin, impatient fingers, rolled her eyes slightly and shrugged.

"Oh, I can't understand him at all ... he's got no ambition, not a scrap ... quite content to jog along getting nowhere," she complained. When Joan wasn't complaining about Jack's pedestrian aims she was bright and amusing, good company, quite kind. But over the years the recounting to her friends of the list of his failings had rather crowded out the charm, and her voice taken on a discontented whine when she talked of the things and services he could not provide. The others sighed mentally. It was not only Phyllis and Kate and Nell who were sorry for Jack Carter. There was general sympathy and liking among the neighbours for the mild-mannered schoolmaster who was always ready to offer a helping hand in a local crisis, if only for the simple reason that since he spent so much time out among his vegetables or working in the potting shed by the back gate, away from the carp of Joan's tongue, he was always the first to hear of trouble. It had been noticed, though, that over this past summer Jack had been seen less often about his do-it-yourself jobs and there had been conjecture among some that he had lost heart. Others more observant, knew that he had taken to having coffee at odd times in The Green Kettle cafe.

Tonight the note of annoyance that soured Joan's voice was because a promoted post had recently fallen vacant and Jack had not even stirred himself to apply for it.

"Says he'd rather stay in the classroom. Sounds all very fine ... duty to the kids and all that. But what about his duty to me? And another thing ... he's got young Barbara thinking the same way ... y'know, that getting-on doesn't matter ... noble ideas about everything being more important than money and a bit of push." Joan bit her lip and smoothed back her dark hair. "It's all off with Charles. Did I tell you? Yes ... and that looked so promising too. Now she's seeing that Con Barclay."

Charles was a trainee solicitor, Con Barclay the son of the small-holding family at the tail end of the town. He was a general favourite locally while Charles Kington was not. But the women now nodded sympathetically, partly because, as mothers, they had a sneaking if disinterested understanding of Joan's strivings for Barbara. They preferred the market gardener, but they didn't go in for discord at the bee and certainly wouldn't have spoiled their opening evening with more than a murmur that Barbara could do worse than Con.

"Talking of Barbara, did she enjoy herself in Cornwall?" asked Kate, ever the pacifier. And the conversation changed direction to holidays just past, the price of smoked bacon in the supermarket, and the new hotel recently opened in Crampton Netherby.

They had all been to 'The Savoury Duck' for coffee or bar meals, except Nell, and she had heard enough about it from the family at home to be able to chip in quite intelligently about the tariff, decor and service at the new place.

"Saw your brother-in-law hard at it there on Tuesday night, Kate," remarked Phyllis, with no intention of hurting or offending her friend. For Kate's worry over Denny, the 'hard-at-it' brother-in-law who lived with her and her husband, was a matter of concern to them all. Month by month they had watched her grow thinner, greyer of hair and face, with the wondering whether there would ever be an end to Denny's folly and excesses.

When he was younger, there had been schoolboy misdemeanours and disruptions. Then he'd begun to experiment with drugs, first enjoying, then needing . . . stealing from them at home, pilfering from petty cash at work . . . a break-in at a local garage. Now there was no job. They had sought help and counselling. There had been remorse, treatment, promises . . . but then this last month there had been an assault and the snatching of an elderly neighbour's handbag, and a new court appearance was pending.

Kate's gentleness, and the sheer despairing Christian goodness she shared with a godly and upright husband, infuriated her three friends, who were full of the dark fate they'd have in store for Denny if he had been the cuckoo in one of their nests. But Kate knew her man well enough to understand that even if the boy was jailed this time, John would be waiting at the prison door when he was released to bring him home to try again. And Phyllis, Joan and Nell knew Kate well enough to guess that whatever exasperated relief she felt at his confinement, and however much she enjoyed the blessed spell of freedom during it, she would welcome him back with new clothes, a warm bed and a place at the family table.

"You should stand back from Denny. Let him go his own way. You've done your best. What age is he now, twenty . . . twenty-one . . . ? He's not your responsibility now," pointed out Phyllis.

"That's right. You married John, after all, not a brother twenty years younger!" urged Joan, who would have known exactly what to do with Denny.

"Ah, but John thinks he's his brother's keeper."

And all of them knew that Kate would be her brother-in-law's keeper right there beside her man. Only when Kate was saying her prayers did she ever think it possible that it might be a lack of courage, and not grace, that kept John from showing Denny the door. Now she wound her wool to mark the end of that topic of conversation. The exchanges had been brief since Phyllis's remark about having seen Denny drinking at the hotel, now the moment was over. Kate smiled and asked if Joan or Phyllis had any summer snaps of their grandchildren.

After the round of photographs there was a general shaking of heads over television violence and a resumé of neighbourhood marriages and deaths in July and August. And then Joan was pouring tea.

"Did you know I'd lost my Aunt Julia six weeks ago?" said Phyllis, balancing a plate on her plump knee and stirring her tea. The aunt had lived in a tiny rented flat further along the main road and the others knew how dutifully Phyllis had shopped for her and visited her every second Wednesday. There was a murmur of sympathy and condolence.

"You've been so good to her, Phyllis.

"I was fond of the old soul. There was no one else really ... my cousin Rob ... that's her son, and his wife, live in Mapleton."

Mapleton was a hundred miles away.

"Will you have to break up the house?" asked Nell, flinching at a fleeting vision of ever having such a task in the confusion of her sister's slapdash and cluttered home.

"Most of it anyway. I'll get started and then Rob and Tilda can finish it," replied Phyllis.

"It's a rotten job going through someone else's personal things," sympathised Joan.

In fact Phyllis had already started on her aunt's effects, not with any other aim at first than to get a difficult job well started for Rob and Tilda. But then she had found the pearls. And they had been on her mind ever since. They were in a chamois-lined case; a little dull from lack of wear against the warmth of Aunt Julia's skin, but beautiful. They had been a silver-wedding gift many years before from a husband well able to mark the occasion handsomely.

Her aunt had talked of the pearls and shown them to Phyllis once, a year or two ago, and said, "Rob's Tilda will have those when the time comes. She doesn't have much jewellery so she'll appreciate them all the more," and she had run arthritic fingers along the small gradations, then carefully laid them back in the case and snapped it shut.

"Yes," said Kate now. "it's a sad job. When someone dies all their things seem to be in a kind of limbo . . . between owners, y'know . . . looking for a home. I remember looking at my mother's bits and pieces . . . shedding a few tears over them. Even quite valuable things looked a little pathetic."

"There's a pearl necklace at Aunt Julia's flat. It's beautiful," said Phyllis casually. Yes, it was beautiful, she thought, and it would soon have taken on its lustre against her own creamy neck. With her black velvet dress, perhaps.

"It's to go to Tilda, of course . . . at least, I suppose it will." She covered herself with that remark . . . just in case, in the end, the pearls were not destined for her cousin's wife.

Kate and Joan were collecting the cups and saucers and putting them on the trolley and so missed the remark but Nell who, perhaps because she talked less, often heard more, caught it, and wondered.

The trolley was wheeled away, there was a bundling up of needlework and a scribbling in diaries to make the next date. And then they were in the porch turning up collars against the wind that scuttled the autumn leaves around their feet . . .

"Thanks Joan. Lovely to be started again."

"See you in a fortnight at Kate's."

*

But it was, after all, less than a week later, on the following Saturday that they met again. At Denny's funeral. On the night following the bee he had climbed into Kate's car outside The Savoury Duck and roared it into a telegraph pole on an empty road.

Nell stood beside Phyllis and Joan, small, insignificant, wheezing a little, determined to support Kate, but worried that the family at home would be wandering in from their various areas of chaos, looking for lunch.

*

Phyllis insisted on having them next at her house, instead of Kate's.

"You've other things on your mind, love," she had said on the 'phone. "But you will come, won't you? Don't sit and brood."

So they were among the smoked glass and soft leather depths of Phyllis's home for the next bee. They remarked on the good turn-out of neighbours and friends at the funeral, and how well the vicar had taken a difficult service, and chosen "Rock of Ages" so wisely for the hymn. It was appalling, they agreed, how suddenly even a young man like Denny could be taken. They did not remark that Kate's problem had been taken with him. She was subdued but they noticed that her colour was better and that she'd had her hair rinsed.

"That was for the Parents' Night," confessed Kate. "You know what the youngsters are like about how one looks, whatever guys they are themselves," and she smiled slightly.

"Oh, Parents' Nights!" groaned Joan. "I hate those ... Jack's so wet with parents ... far too soft with what he says about their precious offspring. No wonder they all say 'what a nice man Mr. Colby is ... what a good teacher Mr. Colby is!' And every year with a new crop of Chiefs around, there he is, still just an Indian. And he takes so long with each parent. I spend the time just drifting around on my own. There was one funny thing this time, though, poor old Jack," and Joan laughed at the recollection ... "You know that tall red-haired girl in Maths ... new teacher last year? Well, she was seeing parents in the same classroom. I heard one father leaving Jack to go and see her. 'I'll have a word with *Mrs. Colby* about the boy's Maths' this man said, and walked over to the red-head. You should have seen Jack's face. Bit out of his league with all that Titian hair and that figure! And the clothes from that boutique in Crampton. *Mrs. Colby,* for goodness' sake!" and Joan squealed with mirth again at the memory of Jack's discomfiture.

There was a moment's silence that the others understood instantly ... even Nell, from remarks heard at home. Then like three pebbles thrown into a pool at the same moment, three remarks fell into the hush, irrelevant, hasty and too loud.

And now Joan knew too.

The flow of conversation after that, closed over the black swirl that frightened her and, although the ripples came and went uneasily through the rest of the evening, the others diverted the chat into safer channels.

"Is that the dress you bought in the boutique at Christmas, Phyllis? It's beautiful." Kate had been puzzled by the wearing of the velvet dress, for usually they socialised in pretty blouses or simple wool shirtwaisters. But Phyllis had gone overboard tonight ... unless ... but, no, she wouldn't have worn black for Denny. No, Kate didn't quite understand.

But Nell, in the small chair in the corner, understood. She had guessed from the moment Phyllis had met her at the door, but had kept her guess to herself without comment. It was Kate who spoke of the pearls.

"Phyll, the pearls, they're beautiful!" she said warmly. Phyllis flushed. She had tried to put it out of her mind that she'd mentioned the necklace last time. So much had happened. They surely wouldn't remember.

"Aunt Julia would have wanted me to have them. They were hers, y'know. We've been so close. I was like a daughter really when Rob and Tilda were all those years in Australia. Aunt Julia scarcely knew Tilda." Besides, Phyllis had told herself, Tilda was an outdoor type ... a sporty Australian ... probably never have worn the pearls. Anyway there were other rings and brooches. She had told herself more than that ... that it was fitting really, after the time and expense she'd put out on Aunt Julia: that she'd probably been mistaken about what the old lady had really meant ... or that she would have changed her mind if she'd been spared: and even that Rob had had something like the pearls in mind when he'd thanked her for her help and said to take for herself any of the small things that she could use. That would leave less for them to clear out when they came themselves in a week or two to finish the job.

Then fresh sandwiches, slices of walnut cake, the flicker of the splendid gas fire and the clink of teacups, the warmth of old friends brought relief from embarrassment to Nell and she was able to take almost the usual pleasure she had in these evenings. They soothed Kate who had the guilty certainty that life was going to be the sweeter for Denny's death; and they took Phyllis's mind off the weight of the pearls round her neck. Joan was less comforted, for outside this circle there lurked a terrifying void. She knew she would do nothing about Jack and the red-haired teacher. Just wait.

The diaries out, the coats on, Phyllis's porch light snapped off and the others took their separate ways home.

Nell reached her sister's home, climbed over guitar cases at the front door and anoraks on the hall floor, and went into the kitchen to a litter of empty beer cans, greasy foil containers that had held Indian carry-outs, a dozen used mugs and instant coffee turning to treacle on the work-top. She sighed, pulled up her sleeves and ran water into the washing-up bowl.

It was past midnight when she climbed into her narrow bed in the attic, the confused noise of the video from downstairs babbling round her as she lay. She was tight-chested and breathless a little, not settling to sleep immediately.

She thought of Joan and Phyllis and Kate with their various problems. Joan would never solve hers. It was of her own making and out of her own personality. This affair of Jack's might not amount to much ... might fizzle out. But Joan would always envy better-provided wives and blame him; or there might be another woman somewhere who would lift his morale a little ... perhaps a succession of them. Then there was Phyllis. Nell smiled in the darkness over Phyllis. She was shocked a little about the pearls, because all four of the friends were members at St. Mark's, accepting the same code, the same rights and wrongs. But Phyllis's solution to her quandary had been simply to re-arrange her recollections of her late aunt's remarks and intentions ... to convince herself that she would appreciate and value the pearls more than Rob's 'sporty' wife.

Nell couldn't help being glad for Kate. Her problem hadn't been like those of the other two, the one of personality and the one of conscience. It had arisen purely out of her circumstances. Now it was solved. Life might throw up others in the future but she was clearsighted and patient and would cope.

Nell was drifting into sleep now, having tidied up the jumble of dismays about her friends, when she had a sudden vision of herself as a woman with a problem. What kind was hers, in this unpeaceful house with its noise and disorder. It didn't arise from conscience (unless it was too sharp a conscience). Was it personality? Was she doomed to endure it for ever because she was what she was? Or was it circumstances?

She did not sleep after all, for a small excitement agitated her until the first greyness of dawn seeped into the room. She calculated, and she wondered for the first time, if her asthma would be any worse if she was in a light job somewhere, than here drowning herself in six heedless lives.

Next day she walked round to see Phyllis and ask what was happening about finding a new tenant for Aunt Julia's little flat.

The Year of the Snake

It was nearly thirteen years since the Chin brothers had quarrelled. That had been during the last Year-of-the-Snake. Before that the two had been inseparable. They were identical twins and they had occupied a corner through-and-through furniture shop-factory which their long-dead father had established. It had double entrances facing out on to the two streets Jalan Kiri and Jalan Kanan (Left and Right Streets) which formed a junction, and it enclosed old Mat Razi's small tailoring business which sat directly on the corner. In those earlier days the Chins had cast covetous eyes on the tailor's shop area, which, if they had owned it, would have given them useful extra space. But, even yet, old Razi was cutting and stitching and seemed likely to persist until he was a hundred.

In the common premises at the back, the Chins' joint, noisy family had been conceived, had slept, eaten and played together as if it was one. "The Double Chins" a waggish expatriate friend of their father's had called them once, and in those happy days the name had stuck.

No one could really remember what the disagreement had been about, not even the two men themselves, something trivial perhaps, but it had led to more bitter thrusts than the usual high-pitched wordy arguments; and not all the intervening, heart-softening Chinese New Year's celebrations had brought them together again. Time instead had sealed them more firmly than ever from each other in their now quite separate businesses.

After the quarrel they had determinedly built a wall across between the two ends of the premises, leaving them with divided houses at the rear and shop fronts obstinately facing away from each other into Jalan Kiri and Jalan Kanan. The only matter on which they, or rather their lawyers, had agreed was the scrupulous portioning out of capital, savings, raw material and accommodation. After that it was each Chin for himself, and they had soon become known in the neighbourhood as Chin Kiri and Chin Kanan.

Not so easily split into two was the twins' mother, Madam Chin, who resolutely refused to take sides, had two small rooms built upstairs to straddle the dividing wall below, and came down with devastating fairness to visit each family on alternate Wednesdays and Sundays. Madam Chin was able to be independent in this way because the astute little man whose widow she was had not only left her with the security of regular interest on a small sum to keep a roof over head, but had also given her, early in their marriage, a valuable jade ornament. The worth of these two securities he had kept back from his sons so that they would have to apply themselves to their work, as he had had to do, to make their business prosper.

She was a shrewd old woman, not so spry as she had been before the arthritis had crept into her bones, but with a sharp mind still. Behind the brave face and slightly brittle manner which she put on along with her best dress for her weekly visits downstairs, she hid a great sadness of heart that there could be this rift in the family that she and her husband had reared with such affection and care. She knew each of the families intimately and loved them all, her sharp eyes open to all their faults and virtues. She was brisk, scolding and generous to them all without favouritism.

But after one of her visits she would sit at perhaps her left-hand window looking into Jalan Kiri with a chilled heart. Out there on the wide pavement would be one son with his wife and all his children chattering and gesticulating as they worked, heating the lengths of cut rattan cane, then lashing them into chairs and tables with strips of its smooth bark. The youngest children would be fetching and carrying, the middle ones, deft with their supple wrists, stirring and applying varnish, poking it into the notched joints of the finished frames, and the older ones would be stacking the completed furniture inside the store or on to their small delivery truck. Their father would bond melamine to table-tops and show prospective customers round his goods. He would talk quality and discount, enquiring carefully about prices round the corner at his brother's establishment and undercutting them a little if the other shop had been visited first.

Then Madam Chin would walk to her other window and look on to Jalan Kanan as if it was a mirror of the other, with exactly the same deft twisting, binding, varnishing and stacking of rattan going on there.

She was a strong-willed old woman but her sons had inherited her will and she had long ago stopped trying to bring them together by direct appeal. She was eighty-four now and she could only sigh and, for comfort, handle the jade apples on a silver stalk, which her husband had given her when she had borne him his twin sons. She remembered how his small cheerful eyes had twinkled when he put them on the table by her bed.

"See what her sons have brought for my little Serpent," he said. She had been born in China in the last Year-of-the-Snake of the old century and when her husband was lost for an endearment as he often was, he would remember her birth year and make the word 'serpent' sound like a benediction. He had had his few short years of schooling at a small China Inland Mission-house and had thought the apples for his little 'serpent" a good Biblical joke, as well as a wise investment. The little apples were still together on their stem, but alas for the twins that had brought them!

Although their lives, as well as their shops, faced in opposite directions, somehow very little that went on in the life or business of one brother escaped the other's notice. Every price, every new design, supplier, cushion pattern or customer was viewed with suspicion, and such was their steely rivalry that they had undoubtedly the keenest prices in the town and consequently the biggest clientele in the low-cost furniture market. Competition in everything was their watchword. If one wife had a new outfit the other was sent packing to the nearest shopping complex to match it or top it for quality.

Now it happened that the two third children in each family were exactly the same age, Chin Tan of Jalan Kiri and Chin Susi of Jalan Kanan. It happened also that when the two of them went at first to the local school they were, term after term, top-equal pupils of their class. Then at nine years old Tan faltered and took to badminton, and twice in examinations Susi came ahead of him. Tan's father promptly removed him from that school and sent him to an English-medium boys' establishment where the masters stood no nonsense; and Susi's father, not to be outdone in the matter of paying fees, sent her to the nuns of "The Good Shepherd Convent" where she romped through each form in turn, at the head of her class. As their 'teen years went by, each father heard on good authority that Tan was proving to be a brilliant mathematical scholar and that Susi was already a fluent linguist. As their schools were at opposite ends of the town and there was cold war in their homes, the two saw each other only at a distance.

The other children in each family showed more signs of business acumen than scholarship, and anyway had no counterpart for age in the other household. So the rivalry of Chin Kiri and Chin Kanan was focussed on the furthering of those two academic careers, and there was rejoicing in each family separately when Susi and Tan were accepted in different faculties at the University of Malaya.

Hormones, or the same mini-bus or perverse curiosity may have been at the root of the matter. Or perhaps it was just that Tan's short, sturdy, humorous good looks and Susi's sleek black cap of hair and the quizzical arch of one eyebrow were particularly appealing. Whatever it was, it wasn't long before the two were walking hand-in-hand on the campus, and drinking coffee every day at a favourite stall. They left home and arrived back separately, but they spent every free moment of each day together and eventually by the time they had crowned each father's hopes by graduating with Upper Second Class Honours degrees, Susi had Tan's small ring on a thread round her neck and they were planning to marry, then go off to the States or the U.K. to study for Master's degrees.

Neither of them had ever had anything but fanatical encouragement in their studies from Kiri and Kanan, and never for one moment expected that anything would prevent their fond fathers from financing those extra years of study.

But Chin Kiri spluttered, speechless in his wrath, and Chin Kanan raged and fumed at his daughter's betrayal and ingratitude, although an outsider might have laughed to see identical pairs of pink spots rising on two similar, outraged faces.

"Not a cent, not one cent, if you marry that girl!"

"Cut off, cut right off, if you take that boy for your husband ... bad blood ... you have always known it."

At what point exactly the division of family blood into good and bad had taken place no one mentioned. Even the traditional folly of marrying a cousin was swamped by the rage of both fathers.

It was a dilemma for the couple. Susi and Tan were dedicated scholars and they badly wanted to pursue their studies. But they were young, their blood, good or bad, coursed warmly and they did not relish the thought of obedience now for two or three long years, and union later when they were independent.

For a week there were tight lips and rebellious eyes in both houses. And then old Mr. Razi, the little tailor died. Grandmother Chin watched closely as the shutters went up on Razi's shop.

When a summons came to Susi to visit the old lady it was something of a surprise, for over the years Kiri and Kanan had discouraged their families from going upstairs lest they should chance to meet their cousins. But these were not normal days at the Kiri-Kanan corner and the terms Susi was on with her father did not demand the usual show of obedience. She went.

Madam Chin was sitting at the door between her two small rooms, neither at one window nor the other, and she was fondling the cool, smooth jade of her apples. Strange ... she was thinking ... that this should be the Year-of-the-Snake again.

"Sit child," she ordered. Susi sat. There were no preliminaries. "You cousin wants to marry you and you want to marry him. Well, there are good minds and healthy bodies in our family. Your signs are right?" Susi nodded. "So no problem there."

Her Grandmother's eyes were penetrating and she spoke carefully, always balancing each sentence with equal reference to Susi and Tan, and so seriously that Susi was out of the room clutching the jade apples in a silk scarf, before the crafty humour of the old woman's suggestion had worked its way through to the place where Susi's laughter had its springs. Now she chuckled softly and went to look for Tan.

When Chin Kanan went straight from his condolence call on the tailor's widow to the estate agent, to catch the little 'between shop' before his brother could get it, he was surprised and not pleased to find that it was already taken. But his anger, and that of Chin Kiri, when he made the same discovery, was nothing to their separate fury when Tan and Susi announced that they had married and were going to live meantime with their Grandmother. Both were immediately cut off and the old lady was in very bad odour indeed.

Then there was a bustle of crates and vans and a smell of new cut foam rubber, and two weeks later the shutters came down off Razi's old shop. Kiri and Kanan were flabbergasted to find Susi and Tan in old jeans out on the pavement weaving rattan with all the skill their fathers had taught them as youngsters, copied more laboriously but with increasing ease by a clutch of not-yet-employed fellow graduates. Inside, two girls at old sewing machines were running up seat covers two feet square and piling them by the half-dozen on one of old Madam Chin's dining chairs. Customers had a third choice now. If Kanan and Kiri sold a sitting-room set for four hundred dollars, Tan and Susi asked only three hundred and eighty for theirs, and a table for which their elders took thirty-three dollars, their joyful clients drove away for twenty-eight. The young couples of their acquaintance who were getting married came ... and told their friends, while the matter of further studies for Tan and Susi seemed to have dropped like a stone.

July, August, September ... six months passed and while the new shop prospered, takings were falling off noticeably on Jalans Kiri and Kanan. The businessmen in the twins surfaced. In December Kiri went to see Kanan. Soon their sitting-room sets fell to three hundred and seventy-five dollars. Kanan's second boy, who was quick with the varnish brush made short work of Kiri's backlog, and Kiri's middle girl who was fast with the Singer made inroads into the yards of unstitched cushion-cover cloth in Kanan's store. The fathers cut a hole in the dividing wall.

By the beginning of February when the Chinese New Year came round and all three shops were shuttered, Kanan and Kiri, ignoring Susi and Tan, had gone to the temple together and later, amid the scent of joss-sticks and suckling pig, were giving Ang Pows to each other's children. At ten o'clock on the morning of the second day of the celebration, Tan and Susi appeared downstairs with a packed suitcase which they laid on the floor. Susi went forward to her father, knelt before him in supplication and touched her head to the floor in kow-tow. Tan, disregarding the traditional Ang Pow ritual of red envelope only to the unwed, handed one to his father.

By the time the Double Chins had recovered themselves and were looking at the contents of the envelope, which was the key to the corner shop, Tan and Susi were speeding to Subang Airport in a black and yellow teksi with their post-graduate course fees safely in their pockets.

Old Madam Chin sat back. The Year of the Snake had passed. There would be twelve years of other animals before it slithered in again and she would be dead and gone. She was tired. Perhaps she would have them bring her bed downstairs again.

Anna Tansy and
the Tudor Rose

Margaret Tudor stood alone by her chamber window at Methven Castle on an October morning of 1541, a handsome-enough figure of a woman, and still with her old liking for a brave damask gown, but faded of hair and marred slightly in the skin by old pock marks. Through the russet leaves of great oak trees, sturdy as the castle walls themselves, she could see the autumn sun glimmer on a curve of the River Almond.

The scuff of patten on cobble distracted her attention and she smiled briefly to see Anna Tansy crossing the courtyard, her arms full of autumn sprigs and seedheads, the hood of her woollen cloak fallen back on her shoulders ... Tansy, as ever, with late flowers and grasses to cheer Margaret's apartments.

Tansy would never have aspired to being called one of the Queen's Ladies, or fitting to address them as equals, but she had known and served Margaret Tudor longer than any of them. And increasingly of late the Queen (though in truth she was the Lady of Methven now) had been conscious of the years they had been together. Indeed, over her thirty years as Queen Mother, her attendant ladies had, in groups, slotted in and out of pattern like a kaleidoscope, as the various factions of Scots nobles had risen and fallen to and from power, while her King-child James V had been their pawn.

But in all these years of capricious companionship Anna Tansy had been the one single constant in Margaret Tudor's life. More and more as the Queen grew older she looked back, over three marriages to faithless husbands, to the June day when, as a child of thirteen, a rose-gold English princess, she had left her home at Richmond Palace, travelled north and ridden on a white palfrey into a jubilant Scotland as Queen to James IV. Tansy had been with her then, a few years younger, but already a skilled little needlewoman, sent to do plain stitching to Margaret's garments on the long journey to Edinburgh.

And if Tansy had never rated herself upsides with the court ladies, nor even with its dancing or music tutors, no more had Margaret classified her. She was simply Tansy, sewing girl at first, then a pair of practical hands wherever they were needed ... maker of possets, and snuffer of rush lights and wax candles, plenisher of fires and message-bearer; then later, but long ago now, nursemaid to the succession of infants who had lived and died in Margaret's nurseries.

She was out of the Queen's sight now, into the castle, and would presently appear in the doorway. The sun was lowering and it would soon be dusk. Margaret moved towards the fire and held out thin, jewelled hands to its warmth. Then, with little more ceremony than a quick beck, Tansy was in the room. She was a rounded bird of a woman, eyes bright as beads and with skin like the breast of a robin, ruddy from the fresh air she took on long walks by the riverside where she watched the grey and yellow birds darting in and out along its banks, and gathered feverfew and other healing herbs for her infusions.

She carried the armsful of larch and willow wands, traveller's joy and meadow crocus and plunged them into a great pewter jug glowing on a table beside the window. She cocked her head to one side considering the arrangement, then satisfied and ready to turn to her next chore, saw the Queen shiver slightly. Tansy bustled across to poker the fire into life.

"There's chill in the air, ma'am, now the sun's gone." She moved about the room trimming a lamp here, moving a chair for Margaret there and settling a fur-lined wrap round her shoulders. It troubled the woman to see signs of the Dowager Queen's growing frailty. Anna Tansy might not think herself a great lady but she was down-to-earth and practical and never either grovelled or fawned. She had served and scolded Margaret's high-born children in equal measure all their young lives and now that she saw her beloved lady falter, she did the same with her.

"Fie, ma'am, you should have sent for more fire and not let the cold into your bones."

"Old bones, Tansy ... old bones."

Tansy was struck again by the sight of Margaret's thin hands with rings that hung loosely against white knuckles, but she had no patience with melancholy; though indeed there had been much in her mistress's life to make melancholy. There had been the loss of three children to King James, and her disillusion with that philandering lord, then his death at the terrible Flodden field, in war against her own brother, Henry VIII of England. There had been her brief infatuation with her faithless second husband and the infants to him that she had swaddled in tiny winding sheets ... save for their little daughter Meg Douglas. At the thought of Margaret's present third husband Tansy sniffed and guessed that he was even now in the company of his light o' love. Loss ... loss ... loss, for Margaret Tudor, of all her children in the end, for she scarcely saw those of her soured new marriage, and the other two that had survived had been taken from her, the little King James in the vexing squabbles among his Scottish Earls; and his half-sister Margaret Douglas carried off by her father, the Queen's second husband, to live at the English court. Faith! Life had been sore on Margaret Tudor, Anna Tansy thought, as she put out a stool for her lady's feet.

For her part, Margaret watched the serving-woman as she whisked the room into comfort, tweaking at wall-hangings, tending the hearth, sending a boy at the door for a warming cup of ale and honey.

"Your life has ever been more worth than mine, Tansy." Margaret gazed at the fire as she spoke. "I never worked for the care of a single creature ... nor even pleased any of my husbands enough to keep them to me. Your man never strayed."

"Most men stray, madam," Tansy soothed, although she was comfortably certain that her bluff Hugh, of fond memory, who had clattered cheerfully from his gatehouse up to their tiny chamber and into her arms every night for thirty years, had never gone to any other woman. The Queen was not soothed.

"And your work, Tansy, was always what it should have been. Your stitches were the smallest ever and you kept the children obedient and well content ... I was brought to marriage with the King to bring Scotland and England close together. It was my father's wish. And yet they seem farther apart then ever." She sipped the tassie of honeyed ale. "Thistle and Rose" they called the King and me, do you remember, Tansy? A pretty notion but vain, Tansy, vain."

Tansy was not a simpleton.

"If I was more success than you think yourself to have been, my lady, it was because I attempted less. Saving your pardon ma'am, but if I had been the king's bride with the great duties, think you that I would have politicked any better? And had you but fed syrup to the children's ills or put fronds in a jug, would you not have done that as well as I?" The Queen was warm now and drowsing. She sighed.

"But that wasn't the way of it, Tansy. I'll come to death and my two countries will still be at each other's throats. I failed ... everything lost."

But the failing that Margaret Tudor meant was not the failing that Anna Tansy saw. The Queen (for she would never be other to Tansy) was in an uneasy sleep now and the woman drew the wrap closer round the drooping shoulders.

A few weeks later Margaret Tudor was dead.

*

Yet another of the sorrows that Margaret took to the grave was that, although her son James V had sired a clutch of healthy children out of wedlock, he had thus far been denied lusty legitimate princes. There were certainly two frail touty infants in his nursery now but doctors had shaken warning heads over them. During the comings and goings surrounding his mother's kisting and burial the King had seen his one-time nurse, been reminded of her love-scolding and the sensible hand on him and his sister, Margaret Douglas, and accordingly transplanted the still vigorous Tansy to his own quarters to try to put some heart into his ailing sons.

But even if she could have worked that miracle, her coming was too late and before the year was out they too were gone of a sudden fever.

For months Tansy grieved over them with their mother, the tall young Mary de Guise, but, now towards the autumn of 1542, there was new hope in the Royal family, for the Queen was with child again and had not sickened at all during this pregnancy. The prospect of another Prince for Scotland cheered even King James, pre-occupied though he was with the thunder-clouds of war rolling towards the Border from his uncle, English Henry.

On November 24th the King's army met the English at Solway Moss, a mismatch of a battle that was quickly and hopelessly lost. A stricken James rode through the grey winter mists to his Queen, now near her time at Linlithgow. He stayed a week with her, and then went to lick his wounds at quiet Falkland. In the first week of December their baby was born. His heartbreak compounded, that fate had not sent him a princeling but only a little daughter, James turned his face to the cold palace wall and, in a week, young Mary was Queen of Scots.

Again packs of nobles bayed like hounds over the custody, future and religion of the little Queen, first one faction then another seeming to hold sway. Once again Anna Tansy flitted quietly among the Queen's shifting attendants, rocking, loving and heeshing their innocent victim. She would have done as much for any infant, but this was the granddaughter of her own Margaret Tudor and she was fierce in her protection.

Tansy would happily have had it continue so, over all the years of regency. But Mary of Guise, the widowed Queen, was asserting herself, as Margaret Tudor had never done, in her rights over the rearing of her own child. She quickly had about her younger French women of her own choice and had no need of Tansy's soothing presence. But she was kindly intentioned and agreed readily that Tansy should seek a place at the English court, perhaps in the service of young Meg Douglas, Margaret Tudor's daughter still exiled in the keeping of the Tudors there.

It was a strange feature of royal life that those out of favour in one country's court could find haven at that of the other. Within a few weeks Anna Tansy was back at Richmond, gathering flowers and stitching silks for the Lady Meg Douglas ... almost as welcome a confidante of the young woman as she had been of the child ten years before. And Meg had much to confide, for, as her niece the little Queen of Scots, was a bargaining counter for Scotland, so was she in England.

When her mother had cast off Archibald Douglas, her craven second husband, he had taken away their daughter to the court of Henry VIII. Henry was in the throes of being rid of his first two wives and illegitimising his daughters Mary and Elizabeth, so that he regarded this young Scottish niece as heir to his throne. For some years therefore a suitable marriage for her had been of prime importance. Indeed young Thomas Howard who had dared to ask for her hand, had landed in the Tower and died there for supposing himself fit match. The urgency for a royal marriage had passed with the long-awaited birth of Henry's son, the Prince Edward. But during those earlier years there had been a flurry of diplomatic activity to arrange a match to some politically suitable Prince or Earl, with precious little reference to the bride herself.

By the time Tansy came to her, Meg Douglas did not much care who was to be husband to her.

"They killed him, Tansy. They killed the man I would have wed."

"He died of the fever, child. He was not killed."

"Fever seeps easy into the tower," the girl said bitterly, and her fair skin that changed colour so easily was suddenly stained an angry pink in her suspicion.

"Patience my lady; as the Prince Edward grows stronger they do not hound you so willy-nilly towards a tiresome marriage. You know that."

It was true. Edward was five years old now, delicate but alive. Henry could not stomach to think that his son was not the sturdy Tudor he would have wished. He would be king some day. Of that Henry was sure and so Meg Douglas's marriage became a more minor matter. A husband was found for her and within the year she married another of Scotland's exiles, Matthew Stewart, Earl of Lennox. He was not her bonnie Tom Howard who had died in the Tower for love of her, but he was well-favoured, amusing, affable, and she was content. Within another twelvemonth she was carrying his child, with Tansy, moving quietly among more high-born ladies as she had done two years before when the little Queen had been in the bearing at Linlithgow, ever watchful for her well-being.

The afternoon sun was leaping through the casements of Meg Lennox Stewart's apartments and falling on the silk covers of her bed where she lay exhausted but serene, with the boy at her breast that Anna Tansy had swaddled and laid safely in her arms. A halo of sunlight fell on the small, fair, down-covered head lying in the crook of her arm.

"Is he a fine child, Tansy, think you ... well-formed ... perfect?"

Tansy looked at Meg Lennox and at this second grandchild of her heart's darling, Margaret Tudor. She thought tenderly too of the first one that she had left in Scotland, and guessed that both of them, the boy and the girl, would have the beauty of their grandmother.

"A fine boy, my Lady, long-limbed and fair." Meg's uncle, King Henry, had been generous and concerned that she should have every comfort in her confinement; for in gaining his little Edward he had lost the wife he had loved most and was sensitive to the perils of childbirth. Meg was grateful to the King ... and besides, there might come a time when it was politic to have given him a namesake.

"He must be 'Henry' for the King, Tansy," she declared. "But pray, find my husband to see his son and agree the name with me."

Through twenty years of calm and storm, royal favour and disfavour with the Lennox Stewarts, Anna Tansy remained with her Countess, though never quite so close as she had been in the old days with her mother. She watched young Henry Stewart, Lord Darnley, grow tall, as she had foreseen, but she shook her head over petulant and self-willed ways that marred his personal charm and grieved his mother. But he was undeniably handsome and would surely grow out of his follies. From time to time too in the traffic between Edinburgh and London she heard of the little Queen of Scots (now Queen in France also) and she would have given much to see her, for she had heard tell of great beauty, wit and charm in Margaret Tudor's other grandchild.

Tansy was growing older but still she walked about the lanes and meadows nearby on the royal estates and, as she held her brown face to the sun and the rain, and touched the soft green brushes of the larch trees, her mind went back often to that afternoon at Methven when she had come back to Margaret Tudor after just such a walk. She saw her sitting that day by the fire, near to death and she remembered the Queen's regretful verdict on her life.

"... brought to marriage with the King, to bring England and Scotland close together, and yet they seem farther apart than ever ... Thistle and Rose ... a pretty notion ..." Poor lady! Had she lived she would have seen them still barking at each other like tetchy dogs ... and even her grandchildren in opposing courts.

*

1564. Henry VIII was dead these seventeen years, and Elizabeth Tudor on the throne. Henry, Lord Darnley, was nineteen years old and Mary in Scotland would be twenty ... nay, twenty-two, widowed now of her French king, but of age, and Queen of Scots in her own right, a Catholic Queen in a

Protestant country. Tansy herself was nearly seventy, living in a small grace-and-favour apartment in the gift of Meg Douglas. The door of her room opened into a walled garden where the Countess's ladies strolled and took the air in twos and threes and where the old servant was a familiar sight scattering crumbs to the tame birds of the garden or cutting sprays of blackthorn to brighten dark corners in gloomy passageways.

Like many another who knew how to hold her peace Anna Tansy heard much of the gossip of others, looser-tongued; and she knew there was much ado about the finding of a husband for Mary of Scotland that would satisfy the Queen and be acceptable to her Reformed people. Just after the turn of the year, in a spell of warm winter sunshine, Tansy noticed that the groups of exercising ladies were suddenly bigger and their chatter and excitement higher-pitched. Lord Darnley, it seemed, was gone to Scotland and if not actually invited to present himself for inspection, certainly intent on offering himself as a suitor. And Tansy's heart warmed when before the spring bulbs were up and the trees a-bud, the news trickled back that for all the searching to find a wise diplomatic choice and, never heeding that her own favourite would cause up-roar and dismay, Queen Mary had found her tall cousin so comely that she would have no other for her bridegroom. It seemed that he was as pleased with her, and in July they were wed in the Chapel at Holyrood Palace.

Tansy, frail and ageing, forgot that she had ever judged Darnley vain and foolish, and thought instead of long-gone years and how right it was that these two grandchildren of Margaret Tudor had come together at last.

In another turn of the seasons Tansy was grown fragile, thin as sedge-grass and breathless now, no longer walking in the garden but sitting by her door to catch the sun, and certain sure that she would not see out the summer. And it was on one of her last days there that she heard word of the son born to the two at Edinburgh Castle. She heard too that even Elizabeth of England herself had foretold, a little peevishly, that this child

... this James, born to be King of Scots, would surely unite his crown with hers.

In her mind Tansy heard another voice she doubted any other now alive could still remember.

"... to bring Scotland and England close ... Thistle and Rose ... vain, Tansy, vain ..."

"God give you peace, my Lady ..."

If the excited gossips in the Richmond garden had heard her mutter that farewell, or seen her, like many another born long ago to Catholic ways, telling her rosary beads in the folds of her skirts, they would not have guessed that she was praying for the repose of Margaret Tudor's soul.

Double Take

Bert Daly and Alf Wiggins were of the old school, reliable, conscientious and dedicated to their life-work. Well ... Bert's life work. Alf was newer to the job but just as faithful. Bert had been at it, in one form or another, for quarter of a century. At this particular place he'd seen off six drifters before Alf came along, and in him Bert soon discovered the perfect partner.

Bert was short with white hair, sleek as a seal, under his skipped cap, while Alf was lanky and stooped, and with a straggle of whisker that ninety years ago would have been called 'moustaches'. But otherwise they had compatibilities and complements which dovetailed them into perfect neatness of operation. Onlookers might have smiled to see them passing along the stretches on the job, for a war-wound had left Bert with a limp to the right, while Alf was afflicted with a slight congenital dip to the left. But the smiles would disappear from the faces of such smirkers if they happened to transgress in the two mates' little kingdom. For Bert and Alf were attendants, par excellence, in the Merchant City Pay-and-Display Car Park.

They both regarded their occupation as rewarding, tiring and demanding, and agreed that this wasn't a bad site to work, for although they were in the city, the surroundings were quite pleasant. The nearby tower-clock had a clear face to keep them in the right and beyond dispute with felons ... and the stillness of row upon neat row of cars sitting smugly locked, spaced and within their allotted time was pleasantly enlivened by the rush and chatter of pigeons and starlings, even the flashing colour of chaffinches when they flew in on Bert and Alf for the crumbs from their lunch-time sandwiches. Screening the red brick of the railway viaduct to the immediate south, too, there was a nice row of poplar trees so that, on blazing days when the suntraps they enjoyed at cooler times were too exposed, they had shade to sit down with their tea-flasks.

That Saturday was a middling kind of day with only an occasional faint smirr of rain to warrant the white plastic coats (which were, in turn, too long for Bert and too short for Alf). It was neither cool nor warm, dullish but not miserable, just right for the job. The pair were doing their usual choreographic pattern of going their separate ways along the outside lanes, and working inwards until they joined each other to pass down the middle row together, hirpling outwards and with their eyes darting right and left ready to make a catch.

On good days they might get seven or eight. They didn't look on them as victims. These people knew the rules and broke them. Alf didn't exactly enjoy seeing them thrash about in front of him but, as Bert had pointed out early in their association, offenders were their productivity.

Bert was something of a behavioural scientist and had passed on his expertise to Alf. They assessed 'types' and tried to decide whether or not they were potential violators. Some looked at watches and then checked with the clock on the church tower, and had exact money for the ticket machine, or walked smartly away in straight lines. They would all be back in time. Others came in by the Exit, or had to approach other parkers for change or, with never a glance at watch or clock, wove an unhurried, meandering way through the spaces between cars. Bert and Alf mentally marked out the vehicles of those ones for watching.

Just sometimes they turned a blind eye at late little old toddling ladies or men with 'disabled' stickers, who found it difficult to hurry back. Or, it must be said, if the offender was young and pretty, or flustered with a gaggle of children.

There were grades of catches too. Big ones and small ones. That morning there had been two six-pounders, exceeding their span by over thirty minutes and four of the lesser three

61

pound, quarter-hour, latecomers. But on the whole it had been a frustrating day, and it was nearly four-thirty in the afternoon. In the past hour there had been nothing ... only two near misses, tiddlers. One, when Bert had hovered near a blue Vauxhall ready for a kill when the clock hands moved steadily forward on to the time marked on the windscreen ticket. But then a young gent from the Merchant City had appeared without warning, and in two or three pin-striped strides, double the length of Bert's own, followed by what seemed like a single movement ... flashing the key, sliding in and revving-up, had slid legitimately over the exit arrow, free as a bird. The second chance had been Alf's and, although not worth an actual penalty, would have brought the satisfaction of a just rebuke and an entry for the notebook ... something to boast a little about. He had spotted an unlocked car. Four doors with the lock-knobs in the up-position, an open invitation to a thief. But when he had closed in for stern words to the woman, he had found her turning the key on locks that were designed to *pull up* to secure.

Bert and Alf were not pleased with their day's haul and it would have gone ill with even the most delectable girl who transgressed, or the most crippled of latecomers, of the kind they would have scorned to bag on a better day.

And then a frisson of excitement passed over Bert as he noticed a small grey car that he had been missing by ending his pacing along one of his aisles a step too soon on each length before this one. It sat parked far into the shadow of the railway arch and poplar trees, out of alignment with the rest of its row. The only outward signs of the happy tightening of his throat was the quickening step towards the windscreen, the whipping out of his spectacles and the trembling fingers as he wound their wire legs round his ears, and the sharp twitch of his neck, back and forward, up and down, to check all the windows.

There was no ticket at all ... not anywhere.

This was the big one ... the twelve-pounder for not even *displaying* a ticket.

"Alf", he rapped out triumphantly and jerked a beckoning

head. Alf loped over to him and they stood for a moment together, savouring success. Bert bared his head, smoothed his sleek hair, and replaced the cap at a jauntier tilt. Alf seemed to lose his customary droop as he made another searching round of the car in case they were to be cheated of this one.

For the next fifteen minutes they were back on the rounds again but alert ... waiting, never for a moment taking their eyes off the grey car. Then at precisely 4.53 p.m. they reeled their catch, with deadly politeness and a flourish of notebooks; and it was all the sweeter that the driver was a man, a fortyish blustering bully who came across the park hectoring a woebegone girl of about ten for having apparently forgotten some errand during their shopping trip. There need be no whiff of sympathy to spoil the attendants' moment of glory.

In the twenty minutes that was left before finishing time there was only another small three pounder. But it didn't matter. The week had ended well. On a high note, they agreed, as they went to the hut, hung their rain-jackets on the hook and locked the door for the weekend.

Tomorrow was Sunday. They had earned the break, worked hard ... long hours ... tiring really.

Tomorrow they would relax, recreate themselves. They would meet, with their picnics and their oilskin coats against the chance of rain; though, hopefully, they would walk through a dappling of sunshine on their usual Sunday path. They would find a sheltered spot beside the trees where they could hear the birds; and try their luck, eyes alert, antennae tuned. They might be lucky, or frustrated ... get the shiver of excitement, or just have to bear their souls in patience. But, whatever else, they would relax.

And, of course, they would have their rods. For tomorrow was Sunday. And Sundays they went fishing.

The Bersanding

The girl Rohani sat on the bottom step of the four which led up to her stilted hut-house in the Kampong Mela-Mela. Scraggy fowls scratched under the house and a cat lay along the low branch of a tree, its green slit eyes observing the scene without interest, between slow, occasional blinks. It was after four now. The sun grew gentler and the women who had slept the hot, sapping hours away began to come to the doorways of their huts to ask a cure for backache or tattle to each other of the latest self-willed girl who had flouted her parents and chosen her own husband. From other huts came the sweet smell of coconut oil or the thud of chopper on chicken bones.

Then for a moment the gossip stopped and the chickens fluttered away from the feet of Rohani's four-year-old brother Jusof, as he erupted round the corner of the hut, howling that he had fallen.

"There's blood!" he wailed and pointed to his knee. The women turned to each other again when they saw that he had suffered no worse than a scratch.

"Aiya, blood lah!" Rohani exclaimed and gathered him into her arms, on to the yellow sarong that Noor liked. "Aiya, there's a strong little man lah. Don't cry now. It soon heal up." She rocked him as their mother would have done had she been there, and not gone over to see old Cik Jariah about the marriage chairs for Rohani's bersanding next Saturday. Rohani pouted at the thought of her wedding. It was all a game for the adults really. They chose the partners, they invited the guests, they brushed and cooked and decorated, and arranged for the rebana band. A great day of it they made with their fine clothes and all! One great day. And then they left a girl and boy with years and years of ordinary days to live out with partners they had scarcely known, if they were good like the Qu'ran said. She thought of her friend Fathima, forced by her determined mother to that hateful Hussein with the fancy-painted hut and the only T.V. in the kampong. Her mother had looked on, smug and satisfied, that day of the bersanding and then dropped dead before a month, so that she never saw Fathima grow pale and miserable under her married thatch.

Rohani put her pointed little chin on Jusof's head, but he was soothed now and impatient, and he wriggled free, scattering the chickens who were assembled and pecking peacefully again.

All through the sitting and the comforting, the squawking and the gossiping, and all through the remembering about Fathima, Rohani's arms and legs and lips had moved, but never once her eyes. She was waiting, watching for a sign that came to her nearly every day, if all was clear. Her work was near the kampong, in Chai Tong's mini-market, and was over for the day by four. She watched then, around five o'clock, for Noor's red handkerchief tied to a bush and fluttering at the far side of the kampong, where the stream trickled past their secret together-place among the reeds. She hoped her mother would not meet her there today, for it was so near Cik Jariah's hut.

At last she saw the handkerchief and she wanted to stand up and shout that Noor-bin-Aziz loved her, that she loved him and that now she was going to him. But she did not. Her glance round seemed casual, but deep in the eye of her mind she pinned each woman to her place, as if she was putting drops of camphor on a butterfly. And she willed them not to notice that she, Rohani-binti-Ahmad, was off somewhere yet again around five o'clock, and guess that she had a lover, and her pledged marriage but a week away. So she rose quietly and sauntered past the bunga-raya bush and skirted the children playing badminton over the line where her mother dried her washing. Slowly she passed the men bathing at the stand-pipe, but she did not stop to have a word with her First Uncle screwing water from his sarong, or her Second Uncle shaking the drips from his shaggy head like a great dog. She was among the kindly trees now and her step quickened. By the time she reached the place where the banana plants grew thickly, she was running, skipping over the roots, flying to her love like a yellow oriole bird.

Noor stood at the river's edge laughing as she came to him, the water lapping and glistening on his bare brown feet and he held out a hand as she kicked off her sandals, lifted her sarong above her ankles and stepped in beside him. The sun struck a shaft through the trees on to two red boulders sitting side by side in the stream and they sat down, one on each side and looked long at each other. He saw a slender girl with eyes as brown and liquid as the pools of water idling under the river bank. He saw petal lips unfolded on white pearls of teeth and he touched with familiar fingers the mole in the hollow of her throat. She saw a thin brown blade of a boy with a wide mouth and strong square teeth, and with a thatch of hair falling thickly over his brow. She stroked it once without provoking him, and trailed his hand in hers through the clear water. She knew without looking that, while the nails on all his other finger-tips were rounded and well-shaped, the one which had touched the pulse-beat at her throat was bitten away, and she knew too, for he had told her, that he nibbled it at his post-office clerking job in the city.

They talked then of his day with the stamps and the wrong addresses and the fat little puteh woman who bought air-letters every day and sent a parcel to England every Thursday. And they talked of her day, counting out change on Chai Tong's bead frame and selling cheap-grade rice by mistake to the fussy Punjabi woman from the big yellow house on the Ulu Klang Heights. He told her that his mother had burned a black patch in her rice-cooker and she told him that her little brother Jusof had fallen again, and that her mother had gone to old Jariah about the bersanding chairs. They fell silent for a moment at that word, then Rohani fingered the red stones lightly.

"Like the wedding chairs lah!" She sighed and he leaned over to touch a flame-of-the-forest tree growing close to them on the bank.

"And the egg-tree!" He pouted, and she pulled a leaf from the tree, stripping the fingers of it one by one and sticking them into her hair all round.

"My head-dress . . . like a Minankabau roof," she explained.

Then it was time to go, or they would be separately missed and questioned, and trouble would follow. They stood up. Noor stepped across to the bank and Rohani stumbled slightly as she followed him. She fell against him and felt his hands round her back. He had to kiss her and they both trembled. He wanted Rohani to be a good girl, but more than that at this moment he wanted to stay there in the clearing for another hour and follow wherever that first kiss led them. But she eased him gently away and, sulky with relief and disappointment, he slid his feet into his plastic shoes and pushed hers over to her without touching her again.

Rohani went off through the trees first, so that Cik Jariah's peering eyes would not see them together from the place on the ground where she had worn a hollow by her doorway at the edge of the kampong, with so much sitting. Gloomily Noor watched Rohani go and wondered at her light heart as she plucked the leaves from her hair and replaced them with flowers instead. Maybe she was like all the women and looked forward to the charade of her bersanding after all. Then, kicking at tree roots like a moody child, he walked slowly home and sat down on the mat to eat the food his mother had prepared.

*

It was a stiff little bride who went to meet her husband that Saturday. Her face was mask-tight with make-up and her unsmiling eyes heavily outlined with black pencil drawn out towards her pounding temples. Her baju-kebaya rustled and hung stiffly from her shoulders, and because she cast her eyes down as she walked, she saw that every step she took kicked out the material, so that she could see each motif of the flowery pattern. The design was exposed, just as she was being exposed today, out of all the days she had spent as one of the quiet ones of the Mela-Mela kampong. In front of her, Jusof and the brother next to him in age, carried the cane of spraying paper flowers, and her Grandmother, walking backwards before her, sprinkled drops of water from a tiny brass jug to ensure her many babies. Rohani's bent head was aching with the weight of her head-dress and the heat of the bunpiece which lay dull and lifeless against her own shining, bunched-up hair, the hair which, other days, dropped past her shoulders and which Noor had loved to touch at their cool green place beside the river.

Behind her shuffled the kampong rebana band in their scarlet bajus and black trousers and with their heads like black studs in their oval velvet songkoks. They were beating out the wedding rhythm on their tambors and now she could hear the answering throb of the rebana band escorting her husband towards her. Then she saw the small boys in front of him bearing his wands of blossom, and dressed in their smart new blue safari suits. At last she caught sight of the scarlet and gold brocade of the bridegroom's trousers and the braided hem of his tunic.

The two processions met and Rohani stepped to the side of this turbaned prince she was to marry. From the corner of her eye she could see the set lips and expressionless face of a stranger and then her eyes fell modestly again to the posy of flowers in one of his hands. The other hung stiffly beside her own, close but not even brushing by design or accident. For a moment they stood there, together but each alone, like a pair of slender palm trees, near but never touching, then slowly, so slowly, side by side and looking neither to right nor left, escorted now by the mingled processions, they moved towards Rohani's home.

Small boys pranced along beside them. Little girls with their hands in their mouths gazed at the glittering Prince and

Princess as they walked up the steps, shed their footwear and stooped to enter the house. They were led to a dais at one end of the usually bare little room and set down there on the two crimson velvet and white wrought-iron chairs festooned and decorated for the occasion. Martyrdom was stamped deep into both faces and grimly they stared back at the villagers thronging the gloomy little room, sitting on grass mats on the wooden floor, hanging half-in at the door, even clinging to the window outside for a balcony view of the pair holding court.

Old Cik Jariah was the first of the kampong women, wise in mating matters, to put her blessing on the pair. She waddled forward to the garlanded tub beside them and took one handful of the saffroned glutinous rice from which grew the 'fertility tree'. Into the hand of the bride went one pat and into the equally reluctant hand of the groom Jariah pressed another. She crossed their hands to make them feed each other in the ancient rite and the same custom made each draw back in distaste from the proferred food. Then the old woman took her choice of the souvenir hard-boiled eggs which hung in pipe-cleaner baskets from the stick tree, and her crumpled face cracked into a toothless smile of blessing as she backed away to make room for another cackling well-wisher.

In spite of the attendant who flapped a limp cloth-of-gold fan at her now and then, Rohani was stifled in the small room crammed with perspiring people. She longed with all her heart to kick over the rice-tub and the tree with the hateful eggs which demanded many babies from her body to make her husband proud. She wanted to tear down the decorations and the crown from her head and run away to the glade by the river to sit with Noor on the red stones instead, and let the cool water trickle over her feet. But she could do none of these things and she sat on exhausted through the endless succession of blessings. She could see drops of sweat falling on the richly embroidered knee beside her own. Once she heard him ask his groomsman to come nearer with his fan and she knew that he was finding the bersanding as much of an ordeal as she. She had thought there would never be a more trying day than the one six months ago when he had been brought to look her over and she was primed to serve him modestly with the cake which had been to show off her prowess in the kitchen. But that did not compare with this. Today she had stolen that one glance at his set face and dared no real look at him, but she knew that he too would be powdered and painted and she could see the henna staining on his finger-tips as he pulled nervously at his fine cuffs.

When the women were at last assured that the conduct of the pair had duly shown their innocence and obedience, there was a shout from First Uncle at the door. First Uncle was today's Master of Ceremonies, taking precedence over the two fathers who were judged to be too full of emotion on the great occasion to manage matters competently. He ordered a path to be made through the crowd of neighbours and led the pair out to the tables set under a faded canopy. There they sat alone at the trestle laden with twenty dishes of food which they scarcely touched, while the other guests sat down to only plain rice with a scrap or two of chicken, when they could have cleared the nuptial board in a trice.

The bridgegroom whispered to his attendant and Rohani spoke only to hers and the afternoon wore on towards evening. A few of the more forward girls and some ribald lads hung about after the last of the rice was eaten and Rohani was nearly fainting in her layers of unfamiliar clothes. Perhaps they hungered to see the two really look at each other at last, or to peer into the hut after that and watch them disappear into the bed compartment. But these bold spirits were no match for the women who shook their fists and chased them away like so many chickens.

Then the scraggy hand of old Jariah drew aside the bead curtain and pushed the bridal pair into their wedding chamber where the bed with its fresh cotton sheet was the only piece of furniture.

By nightfall everyone was satisfied, the children to have seen the blaze of costume and colour, and Rohani's father with the token dowry handed over by her new father-in-law, which would help pay for today's expenses. The old women were satisfied with the modest reluctance the two had shown befitting the serious step arranged for them, so much more impressive than the unfilial ones who thought they could make a better choosing of life-partners for themselves, than their parents. Even the cats and chickens under the house were satisfied with the crumbs from under the wedding table.

Above all, Rohani and Noor were satisfied. For the play-acting was over and the stiff clothes hung up. The Minankabau head-dress and the scarlet and gold turban were laid aside and the painted stranger-masks kissed away. Noor held Rohani in his arms and together they laughed softly in the friendly darkness, that their secret of the red thrones in the river was safe.

When the last plates were washed and stacked, old Cik Jariah went back to her hollowed seat outside her shack, to watch through half-closed eyes for the next couple to find the green place at the river. Then she would plant a word-seed here and there with Pakcicks and Makcicks, fathers and mothers, that this lad and that girl would make a likely match. And she would sit back and wait for her invitation to the next bersanding.

Seed Corn

The day began like any other. The Old Man had been awake on the chaff by the fire since first light, comfortable, because the hearth stones at his back held the heat, and the breath of the cow tethered in the corner was sweet and warm. The fire wheezed gently, not devouring itself, and he would not need to do anything about it before the Old Woman was ready to rise and tend it. He kept his eyes closed until he felt her roll off the mat and heard her grunt as she fastened her plaid more firmly round her wa'st and screwed back her hair. Then she heaved him aside to get at her fire and set water to heat. He stumbled to his feet, tightened his breeches round shrivelled haunches and set the mat against the turf wall, clear of the fire for the day. Then he scooped two small handfuls of meal from a kist into two wooden coggies, silently handed them to the woman and sat down to wait for his food.

She stirred hot water into the oats and gave him the steaming porridge that would be his only fare until the noon break. She had kept back a little of her own meal and added it now to the sup she had left in her bowl. She spirtled that to a paste then shaped a ball, flattened it and laid it to dry to an oaten cake on the warm hearth. They would have it at night with the fish he had taken from the river yesterday.

When they had eaten, he untied the skinny cow while she held up the ragged hide that hung over the cot entrance and shoo'ed out the scraggy fowls and, after them, the Old Man with the cow. Then she bent herself almost double to go out through the door-space to join him for their day's work. Outside by the wall the Old Woman lifted a chip of stone and added it to a pile, as she did day after day, marking the time when their boy would come home to them again. In her heart the mother knew that he would never come, but the pile was to keep that fear from the Old Man.

*

The Old Man and Woman lived in that part of Scotland which, in the 1690s, was neither distinctly highland nor lowland, even if they had known to reckon themselves among one breed or the other. Grey mists that had rolled off the River Earn winter and summer for five or more years, and curtains of incessant rain that had blurred the rises and dips in the landscape, souring their grain, had isolated them more than ever from their nearest neighbours and made the task of sheer survival their sole, unremitting toil.

They were ageing now, both soon into their fifties, and alone; for in their prime years there had been smits and famines that had carried off all their bairns but one son, and now he was far from home. These two years he had been gone ... since the terrible year when they had eaten more than half their seed-corn and, afraid for the boy, had sent him to the great town of Edinborough to the south, sure that it must be better for him there, away from the searing winds that were battering their timid crops yet again. But the Old Man had not repeated to his wife that the only other soul he had spoken with this two-month past had told him that folk in the town were eating grass and raw birds from the banks of the Nor' Loch and were dying in the streets, so that, like as not, their lad, without home or kin there, would not have survived.

This though, was the spring of 1699 and, almost afraid to believe in kinder times, the couple had watched wintry suns giving way to soft, warmer winds: winds that were gentle to the green shoots on the tiny strip of land they had of their laird, and to the patch of moorland where they grazed the single cow that was the allowed stent for their smallholding. But the Old Man and Woman, with their children gone like the eaten seed-corn, scarcely knew what drove them to the wearisome rhythm of their days; except that it was perhaps to give sense to the fiction that their boy would come back.

That day, as every day, their bootless feet bundled in sacking, they began their work. She threw a handful of seed to the lacklustre hens, in the hope of an egg to bind their oats into something meagrely different from brose or oatcake. She milked the cow, while he firmed the high baulk they had made to temper the weather to their rig, troubled a little as he worked by the tight pains as he had now, from time to time, across his breast. They weeded and they cast off stones that had worked their way to the surface. In silence, save for the plaint of a whaup, they turned peat turves to the wind to dry, never lifting their eyes to the curve of the hills and the fair, scudding clouds. Tomorrow the Old Woman would work alone, for he had to go away to do his stint to the laird, the land labour that was part of his rent along with the rendering of a small load of peats and the maintaining of his doo'cot.

It was after they had drunk a midday cog of their beast's thin milk, that they saw, on the other side of the river where it narrowed above a pool, the figure of the chapman.

It had been many a long month since such a traveller had passed their way, for there had been neither goods on offer or much worth of crop to exchange for them. Even the river fish had been sparse to find.

As well as the little precious salt, or the threads, or the dried fruit that pedlars might drag across country on their sleds, they brought almost the only word of the outside world that ever came to the lonely moorlands. The Old Woman saw a fleeting glitter in her man's sunken eyes at the thought, not only of the two-three figs she might barter for, to taste his sup, but of any news the traveller might have of how crops and beasts had fared these past dark winters over the far hill. But even when her own heart fluttered at the thought of company to share their fish and talk of other women bodies, there was no divining that he had brought them more than goods and fellowship.

John Pedlar was well-used to choosing his moment to break

fair or ill news and he did not speak while the Old Woman, barefoot now and with her harn skirt kirtled into her waist, carried him in his fine lace-up boots, on her back across the river, while he clutched a bundle of his wares from the sled left on the other bank. He laid out a selection for them to ponder, before he gave them the news he had brought from Edinborough.

It did not disturb the packman that the old couple did not utter shouts of joy or gratitude that their son was not only alive, not only had heard of reviving crops at home and would be back presently ... but that he would bring with him a wife who was with child. Peasant folk were wary of showing too much gladness or sorrow lest they be cheated of the joy, or were too shallow in their expectations of doom. So the chapman was content that he had brought even a tremor of excitement to their hands and voices as they made their small purchases and urged him to eat with them.

*

After the pedlar's visit the turn of their days was much the same, the rising, the brose, the oatcake, the milking, the hens, and the steady pattern of work on the land ... two frail labourers toiling all the daylight hours. But the hand that placed the pebbles on the little counting-cairn was quicker and the man's step less plodding as he trudged his row; for now there was much more to be done.

They tholed the still-snell winds of late March nights as they tore gaps in the peat walls of their cot, so that the turves would be dry and ready to pull down and stack, for fuel. The other turves, more lately cut and, over the months turned regularly in the peat pile to drain, had to be trimmed and built into a new house. And for that house there was a fine roof-tree which had lain for years with the remains of a long-abandoned home near their own. Traditional law forbade that tenants departing to another place should take away with them the precious ridge-tree that had framed their former home. The Old Man and Woman had never had a ridge ... only a sagging, rough-woven cover to their room thrown over willow-and-daub walls. They had long ago lost heart to use this one for their own, but they had guarded it, turned it occasionally for anyone else who might come to live near and claim it as bounty. Now they struggled it upright against their cot to let the wind dry it, ready.

Only on one day in April did the old man feel the breast pains briefly again. They came in waves, making him sweat as he bigged new walls. But they did not frighten him now. The boy would come soon to put his hand to the heavier work and take on the laird's stint. And the laird, pleased to have a young man's strength, would maybe give him another length of rig and the right to a second cow. The pains died down. The Old Man could see the sky pink behind the hills: a fine evening for gathering rushes to weave a cradle. As her man wandered the riverbank, the Old Woman took some of her wool spinnings that she had steeped in the soft greens and browns of plant dyes, sat down with the old loom that had lain long neglected, to weave an inch or two of the shawl she was making for her new gude-daughter.

When it grew darker they supped a bowl of gruel by the light of the lowering fire, eating, as they had worked, in near silence. Then she swirled water round the bowls and set them ready for the morning. He threw down their chaff and they settled themselves to sleep. Lying there the Old Man remembered his pain and trembled that he might be taken before his work was done, and leave the Old Woman still alone. In the darkness he groped for her hand and she turned towards him. Scarcely a word had passed between them all day long, but now each boney body found its partner, settling one against the other, folding themselves into the familiar moulds of the nightly refuge they had known for thirty years.

The Old Woman sighed comfortably and loosened herself a notch towards sleep. The Old Man grunted, but with satisfaction, not with pain.

It had been a good day. There had been weather to work, the peats were drying, there was meal in the kist and he'd seen that she had still one fig for him, hidden in a corner on the shelf. The pain was gone. Maybe it was gone for good ... or for a long time. Maybe the laird would give them that extra bit of land ...

It might even be tomorrow that the boy would come home.

The Chinese
Goldfish Bowl

At five minutes to four IIIc stood in a ragged line waiting for the school bell to let them explode from cloakroom to playground. Some skelped others with plastic bags of P.E. shoes, some hung themselves by the elbows on coat hooks, swinging to and fro in time to the jawing of chewing-gum. Those few who had any rapport with the establishment chaffed Miss Cooke to let them go before the bell.

"Aw, Miss, gaunie let us go? It's nearly the holidays."

Sara Cooke shook her head.

"You might go under a bus. You can do that after school hours, but not before the bell."

"Aw c'mon, Miss. It's Jenny Scobie's birthday." Sara doubted that, and laughed. At least the exchanges would eke out the slow minutes.

"'Tis, Miss ... honest."

The teacher looked at Jenny Scobie. She was an undersized, thin girl with lank carroty hair and unsmiling grey eyes. Sara had never quite plumbed Jenny in almost two years' contact. Never downright insolent, but dour, and not given to more chat than the bald response to an occasional question. Like most of her classmates she'd never mastered any subject or activity enough to get pleasure from it, and seemed only to be marking time until she was ready to leave school altogether in the summertime. Not a girl Sara much liked.

"Is it your birthday Jenny? Having a party?"

"No."

"Getting a present then?"

"A trannie an' m'ears pierced," the girl chanted off-handedly.

"She's goin' for her ears today, Miss. No' gaunie let us go?"

Sara was saved from ending the day at war with IIIc, when the sudden violence of the bell throbbed through the building. She turned back the key in the door, the class erupted and, thirty seconds later, there was nothing in the cloakroom but herself, the sound of feet stampeding along the corridor, and the smell of gym shoes, an apple core and half-a-dozen crisp-bags. Sara gathered up the papers, lifted the apple-core gingerly by the stalk and thanked God unblasphemously that Thursday would bring the Easter holidays.

The buildings, playground and games-field of Rockbank Comprehensive lay between an outlying city housing-scheme on one side and a stretch of meadow and woodland on the other. The suburb, Cartside, was sprawling and dismal. The green area was part of the policies of Charlock Park, an ancient estate now mainly in public keeping.

Few of the scheme tenants ever ventured past the school precincts to discover the rural pleasance beyond it to the east. The centre of their world lay to the west of the school . . . in a grid of streets round their shopping plaza and the two small factories beside it. Most of the local adults in work earned their living in one or other of these places.

That Easter holiday Jenny Scobie made her own small wage, but not in either the factory or the plaza. Sandra Kelly, through-the-wall, who had a baby a little over a year old, worked in the Co-operative butchery.

"You off the school for a coupla weeks, Jenny, hen?"

"No' quite. A week an' a bit just."

"Will you take the wean while my Mammy's in the hospital? I'll gie you ten-a-week, this comin' week an' the next."

"I'll need to dog the last coupla days, but aye, right y' are. She's no bad your Marie."

It was no great hardship for Jenny to get up and collect Marie on the Friday morning, for there was nothing in her own home that endeared it to her. It was the upper corner flat of a four-in-a-block at Number 7, Cartside Quadrant and her thowless mother, who was as bad-tempered as anyone so slothful could be, would lie in bed there half the day. Jimmy Cole, her Ma's man, would be down the plaza with his mates. The living-room was thick every morning with the afters of the previous night's cigarettes, and littered with the cans that were always still strewn on the chipped formica table, along with the wrappings of black pudding or faggot suppers that made the evening meal four or five nights a week.

Jenny was the last of her mother's family still at home and had the back room to herself. It was the least squalid corner of the house. Certainly there was paper peeling in a limp curl from a damp patch on one wall and the bed was seldom made, for tidy beds had never been part of the household's lifestyle. But she liked to sleep with her window open, and her door closed on the tobacco smoke that generally reeked from the living room. Her mother never troubled her there (neither did Jimmy Cole, which was a mercy she had, over others that she knew). Such cleaning as was done, was of the hunger-and-burst kind, when Jenny herself took the notion to make a clearance. She had a certain natural, latent yen for order, uncultivated by anything she learned at home; and a taste for quiet that her mother, if she thought at all, thought 'funny'.

For the first few days of the holiday Jenny bundled young Marie from next-door into her push-chair, trundled it down the street into the plaza. In the mornings she wandered the walkways, fed herself and the child on a diet of ginger and crisps and sat on benches watching out for anyone she knew, to spend an hour with. The store windows provided entertainment for a day or two. She fancied some of the shoes, and pointed out toys and huge Easter eggs to Marie. By the afternoons, some of the Rockbank Secondary boys and girls had rolled out of bed and gathered outside the Amusements, where they exercised their lungs, themselves and their wit, with a guffaw or two, a bit of horseplay and a comparing of the wares they had acquired in small felonies in the arcades.

Jenny knew two of the boys by name. One was a big flashy dresser called Doug, who was snide and quite funny about the origins of Marie when he saw her with Jenny. He kept offering the girl salted peanuts to go down behind the factory with him. The other was Colin Wilson, a skelf of a boy who blinked at the others through big specs, wore a hand-knit jersey and never opened his mouth.

By Tuesday the Plaza and the bonhomie had palled. The April sun was warm that morning and Jenny surprised herself by turning the push-chair in the opposite direction, along past the fifty yards of school railing to where the hedge of Charlock Estate began. At a break in the hedge there was a path leading towards a wood. Jenny turned in.

The path ran among trees and she followed it. Without the support of the gangrel bunch from the Plaza she was nervous, afraid of being caught trespassing. But she was curious too and somehow delighted by the dim green tunnel made by the flush of budding on bushes and trees. She broke off a twig of beech and stuck it in Marie's woolly hat.

Beyond the wood there was a stretch of scrub land, then alongside a slow sliding river, a field of Highland cattle lumbering shaggily about their grazing. She hestitated as she reached a grey stone bridge close to a scattering of buildings, but took heart when two men working there saw her and paid no attention. The path was wider now, a proper track. Round another bend, and Jenny stopped short, facing a huge square building. It had what seemed like a hundred windows, and wide steps leading up to an open gate and courtyard. Impulsively Jenny yanked the push-chair up and through the gateway. Then she panicked and hastily wheeled it round the side of the house in the shadow of trees growing there. But again she was confronted, and surprised, when, at a side door, a woman in an overall, who was emptying pot-scraps into a bin, paid her no heed whatever.

She ventured to the front again. A car swung into the courtyard. Two men and a girl got out slamming the doors. They walked towards the entrance, pushed open the swing-door, and calmly went inside. This place must be Charlock House, Jenny decided. When she went up the town on Saturdays she'd seen notices from the bus that said —

CHARLOCK HOUSE: Open to the Public.

A man in a blue uniform had seen her and was holding the door open. She'd never thought of herself as that kind of 'Public' before and, embarrassed, she dropped her head and turned away. Then she changed her mind, lifted the chair up the few steps and was inside.

"You'll need to carry the wean, hen. But you'll can put the buggy in the corner an' I'll see it's alright."

Jenny stared at him and at the breathtaking magnificence of the entrance hall ... all brass, flowers and shiny wood. You could get the belt at school for just being in the lavvies at the wrong time, or in some grotty corridor ... and-here this man was as good as inviting her to go right into this place!

But he meant it. She unbuckled Marie, hitched her on to her hip and moved slowly across the black and white checkered marble floor to the red carpeting of the staircase.

Harry Barron watched the skinny figure in black, with the too-long skirt flapping about her ankles, the drooping jacket, the earrings that dangled against pale skin. He always kept an eye on an unlikely visitor and found it prudent today to walk up the other side of the double stairway and linger at the glass door into the main hallway, to see how this youngster behaved herself. The baby seemed content enough to lie forward on the girl's shoulder and, satisfied that she herself was too overawed to be troublesome, he took his place in the front vestibule again.

Standing in the centre of the long hall with the entrance behind her, Jenny could see, through windows at the opposite end, woods and fields like those she had crossed to get here. From one petrified spot she turned slowly to take in everything round her. There were great vases as high as her head and real wood furniture. There were white pillars with curly tops holding up the roof, a grandfather clock with strange dials on the face, and a giant china bowl, high and wide as a dustbin, all pinks and greens, and with a design round the rim. It was the same kind of design as the vases. Jenny was still far from sure that she had any business to be here at all, but when two other blue uniforms came from a side entrance, just nodded at her then walked past, she ventured into the next room. There was a group already looking round there and Jenny latched on to them for cover ... not too near, but not so far that she felt naked.

One of the women was speaking.

"This seems to be the dining-room ... just look at that moulding." She pointed out the fancy green and white ceiling and then admired the long table and polished chairs. But then she oo'd and ah'd over some plates on show on open shelves. 'Plain daft' thought Jenny, for they were rubbish old, and some were even cracked.

Her party moved into another room, a smaller, darker place with a narrow window. There was more of the shiny furniture there and a great big painting of a lady in a creamy dress sitting at a table reading. There were shelves of dusty-looking books and an old globe of the world. Jenny sidled after the group ... more pictures ... one big one of Mary and the Baby. Jenny looked closely at it as the rest moved on, her nose nearly touching the child's toes. She cocked her head to the side, looked again at the baby in the picture; then she looked at Marie's face against her shoulder and thought she was near twice as nice.

It was now that Marie began to whimper and then to wail. Jenny heeshied her in consternation, hastily moved back to the hall, past the tall vases and down the stairs to the front door. She planked the baby into the push-chair and saw the doorman grasping the polished handle. She paused before making her exit.

"A' that stuff ... the chairs and tables an' that ... did folk live here, like in a hoose?"

"Och aye," said the man, "the Raeburn-Scotts lived here

... over two hundred years of them, family after family."
"You're kiddin'!"

*

Jenny lay on her dingy bed that night, staring at the ceiling, puzzled ... all that old, old furniture and books, and the dishes with the cracks, the funny piano. The nicest house she knew was Effie Gloag's mother's up-and-downstairs house, that had white and gold wardrobes and nylon bedspreads, a bar in the sitting room and a wee crocheted lady to hide the spare toilet-roll. And it was clean. Effie Gloag's mother wouldn't give houseroom to yon old stuff at Charlock House. She was puzzled that the folk she'd seen there today thought it was great ... and the blue uniform man seemed quite proud of it. But most of all, the thing that puzzled Jenny was that she had quite liked it herself ... maybe not everything, maybe not the blue china, but there was a kind of shine about the whole place, and it was nice and quiet. She wondered what was in the other rooms.

She arrived early next day and if Harry Barron was surprised (for strays like Jenny didn't often come back) he did not show it, but opened the door for her and Marie and the push-chair.

"I didnae see it right yesterday," she explained defensively, 'wi' the wean cryin'. I've that side to do yet." She waved a hand towards the east wing.

"Take your time, hen," and he deposited the pram in the corner again, while Jenny clapped Marie into position ready for the next tour of inspection.

Today she saw a glossy cupboard in the hall that she hadn't noticed the day before, with tiny, carved, bare cherubs up each corner and along the top, and bigger ones at each leg. She stroked the smooth wood with one finger. Then she moved over to the china bowl. The doorman was watching her.

"That's a Chinese goldfish bowl."

"Go on!"

"Aye, right enough. See there's goldfish painted inside."

"So there is."

"A hundred year-old that is, that bowl. And the cabinet there that you were touching ..."

"I didnae mean to ... honest, it was just that silky to feel."

"It's *four* hundred year old."

"No kiddin'. They've kep' it good."

He went away then to usher in more visitors, and she wandered through some of the other rooms. There was the drawing-room with red walls and white ceiling, a square flat piano and a big velvet settee ... then a small room beside that with not much in it but a painted picture of a girl much younger than herself in a white dress, and a display cabinet that stretched across a whole wall. Quite nice dishes this time, green and pink and yellow. And the library, what a size ... with more books in it than the school library! And the biggest piano she had ever seen. There were flowers in every room too, some fresh, some dried and papery.

A man and a woman were looking at the cloth thrown over the piano.

"That's a Paisley shawl," the woman was saying. It looked old and faded to Jenny but it was nice, all the whirls and wriggles in the design.

Marie began to heave back and forward restlessly, then to whimper, and Jenny made for the front door again. And that was the end of the second visit.

Wednesday was Sandra Kelly's day off, so Jenny went to Charlock alone and, after a tour of the house, ate her crisps in the flower garden.

On Thursday the man at the door told her his name was Harry Barron, asked hers, and called her his 'regular customer'.

"What do you like the best?" he asked.

Jenny considered.

"The picture of the woman wi' the heid-scarf and fur-collar."

"That's Spanish. It's painted by a man they called the Greek, El Greco."

"An' I like the wee cupboard you said was four hundred years old."

"The Italian cabinet."

"Aye . . . an' I really like yon man in another picture wi' the pink cape-thing and pink hat, an' the red and gold tassels on his chair."

"That's Pope Clement the Seventh," said Harry Barron.

"An' all the flowers. I like the flowers."

It was the Friday afternoon that she met Miss Cooke. If she'd seen her first she'd have jooked into a corner somewhere, but they came face to face suddenly. Jenny's face flamed. Sara Cooke was amused and surprised.

"Didn't expect to find you here, Jenny." Jenny's hackles rose. She shifted Marie to her other hip.

"I come here every day. I can if I want," she said defiantly. Did Miss Cooke think she'd no business?

"Of course you can. It belongs to everyone in Glasgow. The family that owned it gave it to the city."

Jenny was amazed. If that was right-enough then she'd as much business here as Miss Cooke or anyone else . . .

"That's Pope Clement the Seventh . . . him in the pink coat and hat," she remarked, not knowing what else to say.

"Is that so? I couldn't have told you that," confessed the teacher.

"An' yon big bowl there . . ." she jerked her thumb towards the hall. "It's for goldfish . . . it's Chinese an' it's a hundred-year-old."

Miss Cooke was impressed. She doubted that anything she herself had ever told Jenny had stuck as tight.

"I best be away. Marie'll cry if I dinnae keep moving."

"She's a good wee soul though, all smiles," said the teacher. They parted but came on each other again five minutes later. Miss Cooke had something in her hand.

"Here y'are Jenny . . . a postcard of your Pope Clement. And one of your goldfish bowl . . . from the shop downstairs." Jenny hardly knew how to be gracious to Miss Cooke. She murmured a thank you and, after their second parting, quickly jostled Marie down the stair. She had never seen the postcard stall in the basement before and a kind of excitement was fluttering in her, in case the postcards would be sold out. She bought five more ... the lady in the fur, painted by the Greek man and one each of the green and white dining-room and the red sitting room, the big Chinese vases and the front stairway.

On the way back through the woods she broke off some green budding twigs and picked a handful of yellow flowers from the river bank. Then she wheeled the push-chair to the paper-shop. When she went home she found a jam encrusted jar in the scullery, washed it out and filled it with water. Then she went into her room and closed the door on the sound of the telly. She tidied up her bed, sat on it and laid out the post-cards. Then she looked round the room.

She interrupted the T.V. just once.

"Gaunie let us put yon wee real wood table in my bed-room?"

It was one of the mahogany nest of tables and had been given to Jenny's mother by a woman she had once worked for, Ellen Scobie shrugged, lit a cigarette and turned up the sound.

"Help yoursel'."

Jenny carried it to her room and rubbed at the wood with an old tee-shirt till her arm ached. She set the jar of twigs and celandine on it and tacked her seven postcards to the wall above. Then she sat back on the bed and smiled. There was a china ashtray on the living room hearth that she'd always liked. When her mother went out she would bring it through and put it on the table too ... at the other end from the jar.

*

Jenny was not so lost to reality that she didn't gather with the others down at the Plaza in the evenings; but she couldn't have said why she didn't tell them about going to Charlock, about the Italian cabinet and the Chinese fish bowl or about the tea-room she'd discovered downstairs in the old-fashioned kitchen. Somehow it was all private, special to her alone. That Doug would have laughed at her . . . or worse, taken the rest there for the devilment of it and gone speaking out loud. And specky Colin would've just looked dumb.

Then the holidays and Jenny's extra dog-days were over and she was back at school. Sara Cooke, given the opening, could be as sarcastic as the next teacher, but not often, and certainly not before the look on Jenny Scobie's face, of half-hate half-entreaty, when she thought Miss Cooke was going to blurt it all out about the postcards. Sara quailed, and held her peace. There was a truce of sorts and, in the remaining term of the girl's school life, the teacher even surprised a grudging smile from Jenny once or twice.

She might have surprised a positive grin one day in June if she had met Jenny leaving Charlock from one of her quick after-school visits to check that her precious vases and pictures were still in place. Harry Barron had been on his way up from the basement after his tea-break.

"They're lookin' for a lassie to work in the tea-room now it's gettin' busy. Did you no' tell me you were to leave the school soon?"

Pope Clement and the Paisley shawl had to do without her that day. She went straight down to the kitchen.

Yes, they needed a girl. It would be just washing-up and scrubbing, mind, and maybe serving teas, if she tidied herself up and minded her manners.

*

It was just that, washing-up, scrubbing, sweeping the tile floor . . . timming the rubbish into the bin at the kitchen door. But sometimes she got to polish the monster brass tap at the old sink and the rows of copper pots that were just for show; or dust the black range that the visitors liked to look at and thank their stars they didn't have to blacklead.

Maybe Jenny still *slept* at 7, Cartside Quadrant after that, but she *lived* at Charlock House, that the Raeburn-Scots had given her. Twice a day she walked tall through the front hallway and along the basement corridor, with the occasional roam through her other rooms when it was quiet in the kitchen.

She had been two weeks there when she was sent, for the first time, to bring lettuces and radish from the vegetable garden. On her way back she came on a boy weeding a plot near the hedge. It was Colin Watson ... specs as big as ever! But he was whistling. That was more noise than she had ever heard from him before.

"You workin' here?" she asked.

"Aye" he said, his face red as the radishes, "been workin' Saturdays a long time."

"Me an' all ... working here I mean ... I'm in the tea-room." She peered at some of the plants.

"What's that growin' there?"

"That's herbs ... parsley and thyme. And that there's fennel."

"D'you like it here?"

"Aye, I do. They're goin' to learn me gardenin' right," he said awkwardly, waiting for her to laugh at him.

"Och well. Good on you ... I best go, they're waitin' on the veg."

She made for the gate, then turned.

"If you come in the hoose for your tea or that ... mind an' wipe your feet."

The Woman in Lilac

I

The black girl lay back on her narrow wooden crib, staring endlessly at the ship's timbers of the deck above. She tried to match the creaking of the planking to a home rhythm, but, as always, the pitch of the sea broke the beat and frustrated even that meagre attempt to focus on something other than despair. She raised thin arms and looked along them, then dropped them quickly not to inflame the boy whose eyes were on them. He would not have been inflamed with lust but with envious rage that his were manacled and hers were free. They had chained the boys because at first they had been wild, savage with outrage at what had happened to them ... narrow suffocating rows of them laid out like bean pods, almost too close to move.

Apa's mind was dark, and fluttered with thoughts and feelings she found hard to pin down ... like the beating of wings when the black birds came at home in thrashing clouds and stripped their grain. There was anger, puzzlement, self-pity, even anger with her mother who had told her so often not to stray alone from the village, for fear of the men from the boats. Obedience had not saved her because eight of them had been taken together, no more than a sling's cast from where her father sat with the other elders, their brows scarred with the mark of their rank and, even as their young were being bundled out of sight, wrinkled over the problem of how to protect them from kidnap. Her mother had been right about the boat men, but wrong about how to keep safe and free.

Eight of them had been taken, but now she didn't even know where the others were. The ship was crammed with strangers from other villages too and she had seen no one that she knew, since she was pushed on board, and then below.

She had smelt death again last night and seen two bodies dragged away to be pitched into the sea. She wondered if perhaps they were the lucky ones. Because under everything else, the heat, the stench, the fury and the terror of the sea, there was the black fear of what it was all about. They knew at home about the stealing of the young ones and about white men who sailed away with them in their tall ships. But no one had ever known why ... whether it was to be eaten or have their skin turned into black shoes for white men to wear ... and no one had ever come back to tell them.

It had been their own kind who had taken them with trips and nets to sell to the white men, and now on the ship it was those strangers who came and went, thrusting slops of food at them and striking the wild ones till they were tame again. When she saw the beatings Apa thought of the herdman back home in the wide land, who'd had a brand seared on him for less ... for driving the goats too hard and opening thin lines of blood on their rumps. These sailors were more savage with the boys. There was the rush of another cane and a boy cried out in pain, and Apa, who had been the gentlest girl in the village, the least fond of spearing animals for food, would have taken an iron in her own hand and branded the man who had beaten him.

Day succeeded airless day, though what was day and what was night was all simply dark and featureless time, marked only by meals of gruel or stale fish or the shifting of dead bodies when the reek could be ignored no longer. The stench of the living thickened, the boys grew dull-eyed and as quiet as the girls. In better moments Apa thought of the free life behind her among the wattle and stake houses, the poultry running free and the soft animal skins that made their beds, her mother stitching at the blue shift she had been captured in, and was wearing now. She thought of them dibbling in their seed, the watering and warming of it into corn if the creator-god was good and sent sun and rains enough. She thought of her friend Lali who had rolled under a bush that day and escaped the men, and who could still enjoy the nights under the stars ... Lali who would soon be chosen by Kis and his family to be his wife, to dance at her wedding feast, to wear the cotton waist cord of the young matron and give him children. She had loved Lali. But now, even in these better moments, she hated her for being free ... free ... free! In bad moments, her mouth fell open, her eyes did not move and she lay staring fixedly at a hand hanging down through an iron cuff, a thin hand that held her attention only because it was in the narrow line of her vision among the criss-crossing timbers, and not because two fingers in it were oddly twisted.

Apa and the rest were not eaten, or skinned for shoes. They reached shore somewhere and, although they were scarcely able to stand for cramped and weakened limbs or to see in the blinding light, they were shuffled into a yard on a quayside drenched with sun. When she half-opened her eyes Apa could see groups of white men crowding round the outer fence of the pen and moving about to look at the new batch of blacks on view. There was a sudden drumbeat, a gate was thrown open and the men rushed in to make the first claim on the likeliest of the passengers just hauled off the slave-trader lying at the quay. Apa was in one of the last 'lots' to be taken, bought for casks of rum and bales of cotton.

By nightfall on her first day in the great America, Apa lay in a hut, feet bleeding from her ten mile jog tied alongside a cart, and knowing now what was her fate. Bound for life to Daniel Lebrun, master of Mount Pleasant plantation, she wept, as she had not wept in all the drawn-out weeks of the voyage, for home and freedom. She had two grains of consolation. One was that as she had been pushed stumbling towards this shack across a dusty square where the cart had deposited her she had seen black children chasing chickens and had heard their mothers love-scolding them from other cabin doors ... as her own mother had done to her in the wide land. The second balm to bitterness was that the skinny boy with the twisted hand, who called himself Toby, had run whimpering alongside her by the cart and was now in another hut across the yard, her fellow slave.

There were yelled instructions, chidings and punishments before Apa settled into the routine in the fields, labouring from the sound of the conch-shell at sunrise till enough work to satisfy the master was done for the day. She was soothed into a kind of acceptance of her lot by the other women who were kindly. But she never, ever, thought without pain of the day she had lost her freedom. She watched Miss Charlotte Lebrun come and go in her carriage and knew in her heart that her own father had been as great a man in his world as this girl's father was in his.

Toby was less sturdy, and slow. The overseers jostled and beat him for trailing behind and even some of the other slavemen were irked that his clumsiness kept back the task and brought down wrath on them all.

There were two other young women at Mount Pleasant a little older than Apa, seventeen or eighteen, each of them with a light-coloured child on her back as she worked in the field; and the whispers of the older women told Apa not to smile or pretty herself at the master, or his sons or the overseers, even for a work favour. Her calico flapped unbecomingly round her budding body, she affected a sulky face and manner, doing her best to keep out of their way and save her smiles for the tight little world of the cabin yard. And two years went by.

There were one or two plantation beatings in that time, but Apa was sixteen when she witnessed the worst lashing she had seen so far. And the victim was Toby, now eighteen and still fumbling his work. He had been provoked, taunted by remarks from one of the employed white plantation workers, stung into raising his puny fists. Other neighbouring masters muttered darkly that Daniel Lebrun would live to regret that he had ordered the slave no worse than a flogging. The fellow had never been a bargain to Mount Pleasant, and now had he not lifted a hand to strike a white worker?

Tied to the bent back of another man, Toby was whipped with a cowhide, until the overseer was exhausted, the slave unconscious and bleeding from the lacerations on his thin back.

It would have taken a bold man or woman to go at once to help the boy. Old hands knew to turn away and busy themselves until the master had ridden off to the big house and the overseer gone for refreshment after his labours. Only then would they come back to the help of the victim. But Apa had no such guile and it was lucky that authority was quickly off the scene and did not see her drag Toby into the shade of the unwed lads' hut, and gently bathe his wounds. When he opened pain-filled eyes on Apa's plain little face he thought he had never seen a more beautiful sight.

*

Apa would just have gone to Toby and become his woman; for a wedding here would be a poor thing . . . without the feasts that there would have been at a marriage in her own village . . . the music, the public declaration, the sports, the story-telling, the presents. But Daniel Lebrun was a strictly Christian man who would not have allowed sin-living on his place, and when he heard that the two had mating in mind he curtly sent the new pastor to them from the town.

This Bible-man himself was kind, and when Apa stood before him with Toby, her head held down in awe, he gently lifted her chin and spoke the sort of words that in future days had him banned from every estate for miles around, and ultimately driven up north.

"Remember, Apa-child, you're as close to God's heart, as much His child, as important to Him, as Miss Charlotte up there at the big house, however fancy her trims."

In the winter their child was born. They laughed softly at her beauty and ran gentle fingers along the two crooked fingers of her tiny hand.

II

1980

It was ninety-eight degrees in the street outside and most of the shoppers who had come into the Welcome Shopping Mall to cool off, were dishevelled, flushed and footsore. But Carla Jackson, having sent her boys off for their lunch-trays, settled herself at a table in the Food Hall, cool, poised and subtly chic in silk shirt, pleated skirt and leather sandals, all in a soft shade of cream that set off the rich tones of her skin, skin that was flawless and soft as velvet.

The boys were threading their way back from different kiosks bearing their trays, eyes gloating over their heaped plates and super-size Cokes.

Joe had wanted pizza, and Seb, after half a dozen changes of mind, had settled for sweet-and-sour from the Oriental bar. In a moment she'd get her own tray and go back to the staple of her student days, to a burger and salad.

Carla looked at her sons, concealing her pride as they sat straight-backed, mannerly, well-spoken and undeniably handsome, with their black hair curling round shapely heads and with clear skin the colour of ebony. The orthodontist had done a good job on Seb's teeth last year. (They had been near straight anyway but Carla was a perfectionist.) Both kids had eyes that shone with intelligence and ready comprehension.

They were into their lunch now and she collected her own. Today was the last treat of the vacation ... shopping for new T-shirt and pen-sets, and having lunch here at the plaza. Carla and her professor-husband favoured smaller quieter restaurants on their own outings but this was what the boys thought 'cool'. This was their outing. Tomorrow they would be in school again.

Carla herself would be back to work, exchanging the jade-and-gold pendant she wore today for her stethoscope; and the Mall for St. Mary's Hospital. She looked at Joe again. They grew up so fast. You noticed it at the start of the school year. Wouldn't be too long before he was going to Medical School if that's what he still wanted. She'd like him to go to her old Med. School. But that was some way ahead. He could change. She had. She'd played piano surprisingly well, considering, and done clever art work at High School and almost agreed with the counsellor on some kind of artistic career. But then she'd made up her mind to be a surgeon. She'd wondered at first when she qualified for the course whether they'd let her do it when they saw the congenital deformity of her fingers. (They'd taken care to have surgery for Joe when he was still an infant.) In the end the fingers hadn't mattered because her idealistic youth, a certain curiosity about her origins and the ravages of famine and disease in Africa had come together and led her in those years to Tropical Medicine and a spell with a relief organisation in West Africa. That was all thirteen years ago now, when she'd been twenty-six, but the harrowing memory of the experience was still with her. She and Arthur dipped deep into their account when there was an appeal; and she had a decision to make in the next few weeks as to whether Joe and Seb were old enough to let her go back to a famine area on a two-month assignment before Christmas.

Carla watched them now and wondered. When she thought now of those months in Africa thirteen years ago it wasn't the baked earth or the dust, or even the swollen bellies of sick and dying children that came first to mind, though God knew that she thought of all those with horror on hot nights when, even with air conditioners, it was hard to sleep. It was the memory of an old woman that truly haunted her, an old African woman looking for help, who'd dragged herself thirty miles from her home to Liber village, sleeping by night under the stars. When Carla had first seen her she'd been squatting on skinny haunches with a dead infant at her breast, patiently waiting for food and miracle attention from Carla that would resurrect her grandchild.

But it hadn't been her grandchild. It had been her own baby and the girdle of cotton cord that marked her a married woman had been barely a year old. The 'old woman' was twenty-seven, a year older than Carla.

"Hi, Mom." Joe had gone off and was back again grinning over a blueberry icecream he'd bought with his own money. His sneakers slipped slightly on the tile floor and a dripping of his ice-cream fell on the lilac skirt of a young white woman at the next table who had her back to the Jacksons. Carla rose with a tissue and with an apology on her lips. The woman turned angrily, ready to complain. Those resentful words did not come. A look Carla had seen before took their place.

"Forget it," the woman in lilac said instead. "Same colour anyway." And she waved a hand at the blueberry splash to dismiss the incident altogether. Carla made her apology nevertheless, and sat down. She knew that look . . . that sudden change from indignation to assurance that there were no hard feelings. It meant "I'm on your side. I don't quarrel with blacks. I'm pro-you."

But sometimes Carla thought that, at least in her life, this was the last barrier, that she and her kind, and such worthy women and their kind, would be free only when they could turn on each other, even have a hearty dislike for one another, without caring which was black and which was white. For a few seconds Carla brooded then, momentarily, without she knew why, there came to mind the old woman of twenty-seven from Liberville with her dead baby . . . she was free . . . in her own country, with her own people.

Carla chided herself as petty. She rose.

"Have a nice day," she said to the woman in lilac, and shepherded Joe and Seb towards the bookstore.

The Late
Sebastian Khoo

Mr. Sebastian Khoo twirled round twice on his swivel chair, ejecting himself from the second spin like a stone from a catapult, over to face the mirror on his office wall. He was apparently quite satisfied with what he saw at first glance. There was the head of sleek black hair, executive-weight spectacles gleaming on the bridge of a good flaring Chinese nose and a benign face blessedly free of worry lines. Then he peered more closely, baring his natural white teeth, detected a tea-leaf between two front incisors and carefully picked it out with the nail of his little finger. He stood back to take another look, but that had been the only flaw.

His acquaintances would not have described Sebastian as the self-satisfied man he seemed to be, standing there looking into the mirror at the Managing Director of Footwear Pertama Sdn. Bhd.

"Oh yes, Khoo footwear is it? Not know him really ... quiet man," one might have said.

"Lives out near Zoo Negara," another might have known. And a third,

"Lost his wife one year ago, maybe one year and half ... Children? ... No idea really. Bit of a health fanatic, isn't it?" And that was Sebastian Khoo in a thumbnail. Many people knew one or perhaps two things about his personal life, but few knew more. A composite picture would have shown him as a childless widower of fifty-eight, living without ostentation but comfortably, in the estate locally known as Hibiscus Heights.

Sebastian's skittish behaviour on that particular evening was uncharacteristic and forgiveable because he had, after weeks of doubt and self-scrutiny, made the momentous decision to propose marriage to his beautiful and inexplicably unwed, thirty-seven year old neighbour, Miss Jasmine Sung.

The late Madam Khoo had been a ladylike little sparrow of a woman who had been an asset to her husband's business career by being self-effacing when she was required only as background to his activities, and by adopting a quiet cheerfulness when he wanted an animated hostess. But she had failed him sadly on the matter of sons and that had been a nagging distress to both of them throughout the thirty years of an otherwise contented marriage ... There were no daughters either; but a Chinese man needs sons, not only to obey his wishes in this life, but to attend and minister to his wandering spirit after death.

Now that there was no longer any charge on him to seek promotion Sebastian had begun to think that perhaps he was due a more exotic partner, old enough not to make him lose face and look ridiculous, but young enough to bear a lateish baby, a son who would arrange a fitting funeral and carry out the future obsequies required for the contentment of his spirit after death. It was while he was thus ruminating that Miss Jasmine Sung had swum into his ken, by coming to live in one of the houses in Flower Lane not far from his own.

Sebastian chuckled like a boy as he straightened his tie to go and meet the lady at The Golden Dome Hotel. Two lunchtime table-mates had been boasting ruefully when their sons had dutifully presented them recently on their sixtieth birthdays with handsome and expensive coffins in preparation for the demise which was now inevitably on the horizon. And here he was, nearly as old, contemplating fatherhood. Sebastian was confident of longevity for he practised yoga, and jogged in the privacy of his garden for fifteen minutes every morning. He frequented the city's health food stores as well as having regular medical check-ups, his father (whose spirit tablet on a shelf in his house he reverently attended to, by renewing the candles every week-end) had lived until he was eighty-eight. As further assurance his mother had also lived to be an octogenarian.

In his imagination, therefore, Sebastian had won the delectable Miss Sung, had sired his son, educated him and seen him reach respectful and responsible manhood, all before he had skipped lightly down the Footwear Pertama staircase and into Doctor Kok's Klinik on the ground floor for his three-monthly check-up and the result of his last routine X-ray.

It was a crushed and frightened Sebastian who walked slowly out of the surgery to collect his car in the unhappy knowledge that, for all the jogging and wheatgerm, his lungs were inoperably cancerous and he had probably not much more than a year to live.

"Best to be quite honest ... a man in your position ... business and personal affairs to settle ..." the doctor had said, and at first Sebastian had wished the good man had kept his honest findings to himself and had lied to his patient through his teeth.

But a little courage came back to him when Jasmine, slim and smooth, walked across the thick carpet of the hotel lounge like a graceful cat in a nimbus of lotus perfume and tinkling gold. It was too late to do anything for his ancestral spirit now, for there would be no sons, but he could make this life go out, if not in a blaze of glory, at least in a flicker of enjoyment. He put his hand over hers and, as they talked, never took his eyes off the rounded toe-nails, polished like pink shells, which peeped provocatively from her sandals.

"One year together ... could make it so good ... holidays at first ... Penang, East Coast, Cameron Highlands, then later ... just at home, music, chess ... quiet together ..."

But his courage was short-lived, for Jasmine had pulled her hand away, horrified at the prospect of giving up her well-ordered life for a few months of marriage to a dying man, and she told him so in no uncertain terms. She did not finish her drink, preferring to take a taxi home alone to cry, and to curse fate at this turn of events. To be wife to a Managing Director

100

was one thing, to be his widow on a pension was quite another.

Sebastian saw her go, then left the hotel himself. He parked his car and wandered into Chinatown. Morbid fascination more than real intent directed his feet towards the only Death House still left in the city, in a corner behind the Sieuw Bazaar; and when he saw the old patched timber door ajar he stepped quietly into the darkness just inside it. A young man was folding lengths of dusty cloth; a table, stools and coffin-stands littered the floor, and several heavy, dark, red coffins lay about in various stages of varnishing. At the back of this area sat one of those, ready-lined with cloth and head-pad. In a room beyond, which was deep in shadow except for the light of two candles, the skeletal proprietor, wearing only a pair of knee-length trousers, knelt in meditative attendance awaiting the passing of some friendless creature with the death-rattle in his throat, who lay otherwise motionless on a plinth-bed against the wall.

However successful in this world's terms, however rich, however clever, if a man had no sons to follow him and save his soul from hungering, then he must come to this. He must be brought near the end by acquaintances, with kindly but fleeting interest, to die here, to be dressed and stoppered, in the paid care of a stranger. If he had no boy children to mount his spirit tablet on their wall and honour it, no sons to mark and tend his hillside grave, nor to bring his soul's after-life needs to it there and care for it until it found rest; if he had no such sons, then was a man's soul doomed to haunt the earth unsatisfied for ever.

Sebastian suppressed a panic whimper. He crept outside again quietly and composed himself for a short while before he was calm enough to enter openly this time and approach the son of the establishment still working about the outer shop. There he bleakly made arrangements for his latter end. It was best done early when the whole thing was still a black fantasy and before he began to feel ill.

"What kind coffin?" asked the pale young man.

"No need fancy coffin."

"Varnish, carved?"

"No need."

"You bring good clothes here ready?"

"Does it matter?"

"Best ... for after."

Sebastian shrugged.

"When?" The young man's pencil was poised. He was not unfeeling but he was being business-like and knew from experience that these things were better set out matter-of-factly.

"A year, perhaps ten months ... when the doctor tell you hospital finished," said Sebastian. It was all there now in the note-book. All taken care of. But it would be a poor sort of end, and aftering.

He moved off again, but not to go home. His steps echoed on the loose slabs over the Chinatown drains. He stopped beside the small arched neon sign which was stabbing the darkness every fifteen seconds, "Green Dragon Night Club". He had gone mechanically to the Death House and now he had come unwittingly to this doorway and the flight of stairs leading to the night club on the first floor. It must surely be that all the Signs were in conjunction, that Fate was taking him in charge tonight, for had he not been born in a Year of the Dragon? He was not a member here for he had never been a 'club' man but he knew that most of them welcomed an odd casual visitor in the hope of claiming him later as a permanent. He went upstairs.

It was a dimly lit place with gambling going on at the back and drinking in the lounge bar area. There were no carpets, only a few worn rugs. He had certainly no wish to gamble for he felt he had already picked a prime loser that day, and so he perched on a high stool and ordered a drink. He drank it and ordered another, and another. He was not normally a drinking man and by the time a world-weary hostess had sidled along the bar towards him, his tie was under one ear, his sleek hair falling untidily over his eyes and he was crying. He lifted his hand indicating another drink.

"Bring two black coffee, Peng. Strong," ordered the woman, and taking Sebatian by the arm, slid him tottering off the stool and over to a shabby sofa in the lounge.

They sat there for half-an-hour and a second black kopi, before they spoke, and by then the coffee had helped. He felt foolish, blowing his nose like a child after a fall, but his head was clearing and they had a third cup, dark and bitter.

"Why you cry?" she asked, as casually as she might have asked what time it was. And he told her everything, from the clinic to the brutal moments in the hotel, from the arrangements at the Death House to the not-wanting to go home.

"Come my house," she offered, speaking in English (for their Chinese was different). She lit a cigarette and reckoned on an easy handful of dollars. Sebastian rose to his feet, almost steady now.

As they walked she told him that her name was Esther, that she had three small rooms where she lived with her two children. "No", she said, their fathers were gone a long time ago. And Sebastian knew that she did not mean 'dead', nor did she mean that either man had been her husband.

From her living-room he saw into the two bedrooms. In one, jeans and trackshoes lay on the floor and a guitar on a crumpled bedspread. The other, her own, was bare and tidy with two dresses on hangers hooked to the window-grille and two pairs of flimsy plastic shoes set neatly side by side on the floor. He made no move to rise from the rattan settee to follow her when she went into the bedroom. She came out again, buttoning her blouse and made him more coffee. They drank it in silence and he grew clearer-headed by the sip. He saw properly the poor material of her flowery top and the too-tight skirt creasing round her wide hips, but her eyes were quite kind. He wanted no more from her than the coffee and the company, but he would pay her what she expected.

"Why you work being hostess, and this way?" he asked.

"It's a life. I have boys to keep. Sometimes I sick of it . . . feel a thousand years old." She lit another cigarette and they sat, separately silent.

103

"Both are boys?" he asked, suddenly cold sober.

"Tim sixteen and Yan thirteen."

Another pause, then, "Would you marry me Esther?" he asked.

She laughed at him and filled his cup. But he went on.

"What is to lose? You get same name for both your boys, legal names, I would adopt them. You need not go back 'Green Dragon'. You have only few months of me, then house and money be yours."

Was he drunk still? Esther wondered.

"And what have I to do for all this? What will you get? You would not marry me if you had many years to live."

"No," he admitted, "but like this I get ready-made sons and you would need promise that they keep my spirit tablet and tidy my grave and say prayers for me after."

"This is ridiculous ..." she began, then answered him, "I would not nurse you at the end. I hate illness," she warned, seeing now that this was not the whisky talking.

"I go hospital when I become unpleasant and I keep arrangements at Death House. But for the funeral ... and after ... what you say, Esther?"

"I don't even know your name," she hedged.

"My name Khoo, Sebastian Khoo. What you think?"

She drew on the cigarette then.

"It's not possible ... to refuse," she said, bewildered at the way this client was turning out.

He then paid her the compliment, unique in her professional experience, of saying that he would not trouble her any longer tonight and would come and see her with her sons tomorrow. Nor did he leave any money.

When Jasmine Sung came seeking forgiveness next morning and to tell him that his news had shaken her into being unloving and heartless and that of course, she would be his bride, Sebastian might have been excused for thinking that last night's coinciding Signs at the Death House and the "Green Dragon" had been, instead, the fates conspiring to cheat him of his year with her after all. Actually she had spent a sleepless night kicking herself, trying to put a valuation on his house and wondering just how much insurance he carried.

"I sorry Jasmine. I promised now to someone else," he said simply, for integrity's sake not willing to renege on his offer to Esther. Thus spurned, Jasmine walked away, angry with herself, furious with Sebastian and sure that he was not only ill in body, but out of his mind as well.

Sebastian was not a man used to making decisions in cold blood. He and his late wife had been considerate to each other and he would have given all to the lovely Jasmine without much return. But both parties to the marriage contracted two weeks later on January 3rd, entered it for purely selfish reasons. Before that date Esther had reminded her bridegroom to see a lawyer about his will and Sebastian had asked, before he made the appointment, for the promise in writing of her boys to play the part of bona fide sons after his death.

The boys were not keen at first to have their lives disrupted, but when the younger, Yan, saw the bedroom in Hibiscus Heights which he would occupy alone and where he could read, undisturbed, the books in the book-case outside his door, he was won. And when the elder lad, Tim, was given the freedom, if he was careful, of the fine stereo equipment in the sitting room, he at least stopped sulking and agreed to the terms of his mother's marriage. There was after all nothing much to keeping a spirit tablet and going twice a year to clip a few weeds round the old man's grave. Apart from that, he would only have to turn up at the funeral.

During the month of January, with Sebastian still able to be at work, Esther found the continual quietness of Hibiscus Heights monotonous and dull. She could see that the Punjabi lady on the corner, the Malay one in the white house and the young mother next door gave little afternoon tea parties. She was not invited but as a newcomer she really could not expect that. But nevertheless she was bored. And so she threw all her energy into cleaning the house from top to bottom, putting back on the furniture and glass the shine which it had been losing since the death of the first Mrs. Khoo. She found a photograph of that good lady in a silver frame lying tarnishing in a bureau drawer. She spent almost an entire morning burnishing its intricate corners for she knew that Sebastian's first marriage had been a happy love-match and not a calculated arrangement. Although Esther would have denied that this was anything more than just another cleaning job, she was pleased when her husband commented on it standing there gleaming on the display cabinet, and slipped down the same evening to the Orchid Nursery to choose for her the most delicate plant he could find; Esther generally liked big colourful blooms, but she was touched all the same.

So touched was she in fact, that she was determined to make an event of the Chinese New Year early in February, for it would probably be Sebastian's last. The boys thought the idea great nonsense and planned to go out, but a sharp word from his mother took care of Tim and the threat of locked bookcases of Yan. Late at night on the last day of the old year they all watched Sebastian make offerings of prayers and meditation in remembrance of his parents and first wife. They ate the festive meal which Esther had bought ready-made from the market stalls and, although Tim was still muttering and threatening to go out, he made no such move. Yan, whose previous experience of the religious rites had been sketchy, found the little rituals surrounding the Rain God, the kitchen God and the Door God curious and interesting. He was enthusiastic about Nan Chung, the God of Learning, but a little sceptical of his powers because, as he had several times in moments of confidence told Sebastian, the doors of real learning were closed to those who had not studied English literature.

Whether that was true or not, on New Year's Day both boys received red Ang Pow envelopes from Sebastian. Yan ripped his open to find a small money gift, but also a note offering him a place at an English-medium school from the start of the next school term. Yan had no reservations about the gift and from then on he was Sebastian's to command. Along with his money Tim pulled out a similar note offering him a vocational course in electronics for as long as he needed to study, but his previous experience of his mother's men friends was bitter, and he had always found that a gift from them was no more than a bribe to get lost for two hours. With that as his cue he pocketed the money but tore the note in shreds and walked out of the house.

Yan thought his brother foolish for throwing away the chance of a useful course, but was soon absorbed in a book and unconscious of the hurt on the faces of the other two. Sebastian was sorry for Esther that her son should be rude and ungrateful and her special day ruined. They sat awkwardly looking into the garden for a time, not knowing what to say. They would not now capture the festive spirit they had planned.

"You like to go out and eat at hotel tonight instead?" But Esther was sorry for Sebastian that his kindness had been flung back in his face. She would go out tomorrow and buy a ladylike dress that would make him proud to be seen with her at any hotel ... no frills, something simple.

"Tomorrow best Sebastian, tomorrow we go to hotel. Tonight we watch T.V."

When Esther was dressed next day in a girlish high-waisted dress that might have suited someone twenty years younger, Sebastian nearly laughed, but something held him back, something that told him there was kindness in her choice. And it was the same feeling that kept Esther from telling him that she was uneasy in the quiet refinement of The Golden Dome Hotel and would have enjoyed The Green Dragon better.

As the months slipped by and each began to know the other a little better, Sebastian learned to forsake some of the hotel meals for a shadowy corner of the night club, and Esther tried to choose clothes like the first Madam Khoo might have worn. She did, however, favour with them all, a long, black, feather scarf which trailed across her bosom, over her shoulder and down her back, and which Sebastian assured her was beautiful. In that scarf she was able to face hotels, neighbours and Green Dragon alike, and even feel chic on the Parents' Evening at Yan's new school.

They were glad that they had taken these outings even when Sebastian began to get breathless, glad that they had made something of each festival as it had come round, because by August, when it was time for the Moon Cake celebrations, he was too ill to go out. But at home Esther prepared a little altar on the patio made from paper-covered cartons and lit with red candles. She hung lanterns and laid a table, true to tradition, with melons, pomegranates, grapes, apples and peaches. Tim was off somewhere helping at a party with his disco and group, and Sebastian spoke that day, for the last time, of the boy's future.

"Not let Tim miss chance of that college. He knows a lot about these things but better to train properly."

Yan, grown tall in the months since January, took Sebastian's arm and helped him out to his chair on the patio and, when Esther took him from her son and settled him with cushions at his back, she was struck by the lightness of his body and brushed an impulsive kiss on his forehead.

It was the day after that that she went to see Doctor Kok and the proprietor of the Death House.

The Moon-cake day was his last festival because by the birth of Confuscius, Sebastian Khoo was dead. But he had died in his own bed, after four weeks spent by Esther in unpleasant and distressing day and night nursing, during which she had left him only long enough to snatch a little sleep for the next day. When she had cancelled the Death House and told Doctor Kok there was to be no hospital she did not realise the burden she was taking on, for one who feared and hated illness. And the surprising thought passed through her mind one day towards the end, that it would have made no difference if she had.

When the undertaker had come and gone, Yan felt suddenly bleak and even Tim was moved a little by his mother's strange grief but he could not bring himself to wail at Sebastian's coffin. He had gone with her certainly to make the funeral arrangements but then had gone loping off to avoid embarrassment by seeking out his friends.

In the early months of her marriage Esther, having no comprehension of what she might be heir to, had repeatedly counted out what the cheapest and simplest funeral would cost, with unvarnished coffin, cheap linens for the corpse and the most frugal fare she could provide for any business associates who might come to the house. She had set it all out in a little notebook which was in her handbag when she went to see the undertaker.

At the hour appointed by the astrologer as propitious, those joining the funeral procession arrived at the house in Flower Lane dressed sombrely for the occasion. Jasmine Sung, attending as a neighbour, arrived while Yan and Esther could be seen kneeling before the coffin in the next room. Having kept herself aloof from Sebastian's new family after her first shocked sighting of the wife who had snatched her inheritance from her, Jasmine now found herself beside Tim in the hallway, not knowing who he was.

"Very sad," she began. "Very sad about Mr. Khoo. Not right in the head with his illness, you know. She was a nightclub hostess, his wife, before he married her ... a fit of depression it was ... very sad. Poor foolish Sebastian."

Tim Khoo turned and looked at her with all the considerable insolence of which he was capable.

"It is my father you talk about Madam, and nothing was wrong with his head. He give me very wise advice about my studies and I go soon to college, thanks to him."

It was the first time Tim had admitted, even to himself, that he would take up the offer on the electronics course.

"And," he added witheringly, "she very good wife, the night-club hostess." He had just time to walk into the next room and prostrate himself with heartrending abandon in front of the coffin, before a dozen or more of his friends arrived with an assortment of wind and percussion instruments in an old van. Behind them came the Manager and staff of The Green Dragon bearing banners proclaiming that Sebastian Khoo had been KIND, FAITHFUL, GENEROUS, PROSPEROUS, HONEST ... and LUCKY. Already assembled in the garden were schoolmates of Yan's with wads of paper images to burn at the graveside.

When at last the procession set out from what had once been the quietest house in Flower Lane it was the costliest and most elaborate that had ever been seen there, and no evil spirit would have dared linger within a mile of Tim's group and its cacophony of drums and cymbals.

Esther was supremely confident that she had chosen her funeral dress with taste and restraint. The skirt fell in graceful folds and the sleeves were caught in at the wrists. She had wondered at first about the plunge of the neckline, then remembered in a moment of inspiration that it would complete the honour due to her husband to wear with it the feather boa he had liked so much. When the hearse, bearing the finest coffin the undertaker had been able to provide, took up its position, Esther moved out to follow it with a tall son at each shoulder. She was just in time to catch the remark from Jasmine Sung to another neighbour.

"One can only grieve for Sebastian's spirit. All very fine to have adopted sons . . . of a kind . . . but never to have fathered a boy himself, very sad," and she sighed.

Esther turned with immense dignity.

"You are wrong Madam, Sebastian's child will be born next April, and Doctor Kok is certain from his tests that child will be a third son."

And with a majestic swirl of her feather scarf Esther joined the noisy and affectionate procession ready to accompany the late Sebastian Khoo on the journey to join his ancestors.

The Deadly Sins
of Molly Drurie

The Reverend Ephraim Dundee did not look forward with pleasure to his first session-meeting at the tiny parish church of Netherton in Stirlingshire, to which he had been called barely a month before, in the winter of 1802. He was young, earnest, kindly, and dedicated to his high calling, and he had idealistic notions of what kind of men his elders should be. It had to be said that, in his first round of visitation to his congregation, he had already met several warm-hearted and godly men he felt he would be happy to work with in the tending of his flock. But that had not been his impression of the elders who had been the cohorts of his stern and narrow predecessor and whom he had inherited, ordained as they were, for life. They seemed to Ephraim to be, to a man, cheerless, censorious and gloomy, and his heart quailed for the hapless servant-lass from Greenshaws farm who was to compear before them tonight, unwed, and already visibly with child.

As he made his way from his manse at the top of the village track he was telling himself that in time he would surely gather about him kindlier, better-humoured and more compassionate elders, better suited to the kind of ministry he intended to exercise. But that would not help young Molly Drurie tonight. From the passing remarks of his Session Clerk and two or three of the others, he had the appalled feeling that tonight they looked forward with greater anticipation to savaging the girl, than to any of the other business to be conducted.

Ephraim reached the kirk, took his scholarly stoop and pale, intense face into the bare little session-house, put a light to the tallows on the wall brackets and set out paper, ink, sand and quills on the long table. Then, since he was as well aware as anyone of the importance in a small place, of knowing who were the fathers of ill-begotten bairns, if incestuous relationships in the next generation were to be avoided, he settled to ten minutes of prayer for the guidance of the Spirit before the first of his elders would arrive.

The Kirktoun of Netherton was small and compact, a dozen cottages clustered round church, schoolroom and inn. But the parish itself was widespread, taking in outlying crofts and farms in the surrounding hills, and six of the seven elders who were now converging on the session-house came from these far-flung directions. The seventh, the Clerk, Adam Pringle, who was also the dominie, lived next door in a room at the back of the schoolhouse, and reached the meeting-room just as Ephraim lifted his head from his prayers.

Ephraim, whose greatest temptation would always be to spend too much time with his beloved books had, at first, cherished high hopes that his session-clerk dominie would turn out to be a kindred spirit. As a divinity student he had been assistant to several different ministers who had found their school-masters good late-night companions over a pipe and a flickering fire, when the shepherding and the tutoring were done for the day. But Pringle had been too long a big frog in a small pond, and he had once spent a week in London which had given him a world perspective on most things ever since. He rated his intellectual capacity well above that of anyone else he was likely to meet and did not anticipate that this green new minister would be up to invigorating or enlivening discussion of pamphlets or the worthwhile dissecting of ideas. He was self-important and dogmatic and Ephraim had gone home disappointed after his first purely social call on his lanky red-quiffed clerk.

Rob Lochrie was next to arrive. He was a well-built man, but grey pale as if he had thin blood in his veins, and he had shifting, restless eyes that seemed to the minister to look right past him, whenever the two men had chanced to speak with each other.

Then there was Will Glasfurd. If ever the fat parish miller was of a mind to be merciful to sinners he was certainly not so on that January night, for the several drams he had taken, on top of two helpings of Mistress Glasfurd's mince collops and dumpling, had given him an unclear head and indigestion. With a surly nod to Ephraim he took his place as far as possible from the minister in order to keep his tell-tale breath to himself.

The Agnew brothers from Laigh Gifford, like as two of their own turnips, coarse and purple of face, and with rough dark coats cut from the same bolt of cloth, came striding down from their farm, arguing. Tammas Agnew, who loved an access of easy money, had, outwith their partnership, concluded a quiet market deal to his own great advantage and had been foolish enough to gloat about it over his brother. And Pate, riled beyond his never-very-great endurance, was swearing angrily in a manner ill-befitting one of the session brethren, as they slid on to the bench at one side of the table. Only the need to bid a curt 'good-evening' to those already in place, and the arrival on their heels of Gib Evans put an end to his cantankers; though the meeting was well started before Pate Agnew could properly concentrate on the matters in hand.

Gib Evans came from a bleak little cottage on a sour patch of ground a mile or two from the village. He wore a perpetually ill-done-to expression on his narrow, bearded face, resentful over his land treatment by the laird and one or two cattle transactions in which he had been bettered by the other party. He was the more peevish now, when he saw that the place the minister was beckoning him to take, was next to Will Glasfurd who had once been his dunce schoolmate and was now worth five times as much. Evans, who had many a time done Will's sums for him in those old days, found it hard to thole his bien company now, and thought the world a queerly unfair place.

Any one of the rest could have told Ephraim that Sam

Slocum would come ambling in at the tail end of the procession to the kirk. He had been at the tail end of everything since the day he had been born, last of ten children, to his exhausted mother. He laboured, without too much effort, on the laird's own estate, where out of sight was often out of mind, and where he could sprawl in the lea of a dyke after his midday bite, thinking, at his uninterrupted leisure, long gloomy thoughts on the wickedness of mankind. He had done so this afternoon in dutiful preparation for casting his stone tonight.

Ephraim Dundee looked round his assembled court, all of them suitably grave and shocked of face for the trial of Molly Drurie. There had not been a smile or hail-fellow handshake among them; no more than an odd grunt of recognition. The minister made up his mind, before he had even opened this first meeting with a prayer for wisdom and charity, that before the month was out he would leaven his session by asking the cheerful cobbler Ben Lafferty to become one of his ordained elders. Then the first matter on the agenda was introduced.

Molly arrived at the time appointed. She was a small brown girl and, except for a pair of large hazel eyes, quite plain. She was neat and tidy in her Sunday braws, her hair braided, her plaid with even creases in it from careful nightly folding. She pushed open the yard door and stood shivering from cold and fright outside the room where the elders were in conclave.

Her own home, where an ageing grandmother had reared her, was far outside Netherton parish, a windswept cot miles from anywhere and from any real experience of life and its pitfalls. She had been hired at the early summer feeing-fair and left home for Greenshaws with a change of clothing and strict instructions to do exactly what was demanded in her new place, and not to come back snivelling that too much was wanted of her. Her grandmother had done her best for her but was ailing to death now and wanted nothing but peace to go into her dwyne without the stir of young life in the cot ... however docile. And Molly was certainly docile. Things had been demanded of her that she hadn't dreamed of expecting and she shuddered, as she had done for months past, at the thought of yon footsteps coming towards her kitchen bed in the small hours of morning, and the unwelcome body heaving itself in beside her.

For over six months Greenshaws had been a joyless place for her. The mistress was a chattel herself, entirely dominated by her man, and she was cold and dour to the girl. Molly's food was sparse, her bed draughty, thinly covered ... and after the first week not even her own. She had scarcely heard a kind word from anyone then until the shy ploughman had started to carry her milk pail for her, told her she was pretty and confided his own dreams of shaking off the Greenshaws dust and finding even a tiny place of his own to work. She liked to think about Malky the ploughboy ... but not tonight. The coming ordeal had cast everything else from her mind. She had lived in cold dread of it for ten days and her heart was in her aching boots when Master Pringle's red tuft of hair appeared round the session-room door and an arm as long as a cart-shaft pulled her into the Presence. She glanced at the minister, and then at the other seven figures, black as crows in their Sabbath suits, casting long eerie shadows on the walls under the guttering lights. Then she dropped her eyes.

Molly was never able, then or later, to pair any of the elders with particular questions or verdicts on her sin, even if she had thought to try. But Ephraim noted who said what on that night and, as he became better acquainted with each, wondered at the dovetailing of man and comment, and learned a deal about human nature in the wondering.

The minister would have had Molly take the stool at the end of the table but Pringle's long arm had shot out to remove it to a dark corner so that the girl would have to stand before them ... not sit at her ease.

"You ken what you're here for, Molly? said Ephraim gently.

"Aye."

"Dinnae be frightened. We're just to ask you to name the faither of your bairn and then do the richt thing aboot gettin' wed. Then maybe a Sabbath or two at the pillar or the stool."

"Bide there, Minister," cautioned Pringle, "best wait and see what the wanton has to say for herself afore lettin' her off as easy . . ." He turned to Molly. "The name of your sinner-lad, Molly Drurie, an you please."

"No' the man's name, Master Dundee, sir" she pleaded, turning to the minister. "Dinnae make me say that."

"It's your Christian duty to speak, girl," insisted Pringle.

"I cannae," she whispered.

"Every other lassie that's in your boots, speaks oot. Are you that thrawn wi' pride you see yoursel' different to them? Think shame on you. A bit mair humbleness would better suit you."

"Or maybe," rasped Evans "you're that jealous of bonnier, brighter lassies, you wanted to be upsides wi' them and get yoursel' a boy, and ken fine you've hoodwinked some silly lad wi' your wiles."

Molly was flushed with anger now as well as misery.

"I didnae hoodiewink nob'dy, I never did!" she wailed.

"Can you no' just tell us the father, Molly. If you're no' able to wed him it neednae go beyond this room," urged Ephraim, though he was far from sure of the discretion of his brethren.

"I cannae tell," whispered Molly.

"You're a barefaced, insolent, ill-tempered besom!" exploded Pate Agnew, "to speak so to the elders of your kirk."

Twice more they demanded a name, but Molly denied them and when they knew they were to be cheated of the name they wanted, there was bedlam, with scolding, scorn and accusation hurled at her from every side, words echoing against bare stone walls.

There was Sam Slocum rousing himself enough to fling at her gossip from Greenshaws itself.

"You're an ungrateful wench, for I have it fae your mistress that you lie abed of a morning instead of having the fire riped and the brose made for the menfolk." Molly thought wearily of the great sickness there was on her every morning even yet, after six months. But before she had opened her mouth to protest, Will Glasfurd, with his great paunch resting on the table thundered another jibe.

"Aye, it's a graceless lassie gets a fine livin' in a place the likes of Greenshaws wi' good meat and sup and plenty of it, and then gi'es the gudefolk a bad name wi' her loose wicked ongoin's, gettin' hersel' wi' bairn."

"An takin' good wages forbye your arlin' shillin' at the fair!" stormed Tammas Agnew.

The darts were fairly flying now ... 'grasping' 'idle' 'ill-tempered' 'greedy' 'jealous' 'bold'. Molly's grandmother, now on her deathbed and past defending her, would not have recognised in this barrage, the placid, biddable and simple lass she had sent to Netherton.

But Ephraim Dundee had had enough. His black-dark eyes blazed in his white face and his fist hit the table with a resounding thump so that the tallows guttered.

"Brethren, that will be enough! It's but a wayward lassie we have here, no' a criminal felon," he thundered.

Molly was in tears, her eyes cast down. But seven other awed faces turned slowly towards the minister in sudden recognition of an authority they would come to know well over the next twenty years. There was a clearing of throats by some and a shuffling of uneasy feet from others who wondered what the world was coming to.

Ephraim swiftly proposed two Sabbaths on the cutty stool, quelled any opposition with a look and hoped that Molly would see fit to reveal the identity of her child's father at some future date. But he, and they, knew in their hearts that if she had not been broken tonight she was unlikely to give the lad away later.

After the minister's heartfelt benediction, the seven rose to leave, each disturbed in his own way at Ephraim's high-mindedness, each directing his resentment in his own way.

Pringle went home to write his minutes in grand, pedantic, reproving style. Glasfurd went to a good dram to chase those he had already taken. Pate Agnew began to re-vent his anger over the sly transaction with which Tammas Agnew was consoling himself, and Slocum reached home and rolled into bed while his overworked wife doused the fire and did the chores ready for her early morning rise. Evans went away alone, sulking as he did after every session meeting, that the others were all so much better set up in life than he was himself.

As the minister had tidied up his papers and watched his elders scale, he had felt that he himself had been blooded and that he had come through, now having the measure of his men. Except perhaps of big Rob Lochrie ... for, of all seven, only Lochrie had held his tongue from lashing the girl. That had been a puzzle to Ephraim for he had not greatly taken to the man the few times they had met. Perhaps somewhere there was a kinder streak in him than in the others. The elder disappeared through the doorway and the minister had a last quiet word with Molly before he saw her out, locked up the session-house door and took the path through his glebe to the manse.

Molly happed herself warmly in her plaid and set out for Greenshaws, thankful that the spiering was done and that she had held her peace. She passed through the Kirktoun. Then beyond the last cottage a tall figure unfolded from the dark shadows that fell round an ancient tree, and a hand touched her shoulder. She shook it off, but not with fright, for she had expected to find the man there. She stood before him, the moonlight streaming down on her set face, and she held out her hand. Silently he drew out a small leather draw-string purse and there was a jingle of coins in it as he handed it over.

"I very-near cliped on you," she said, more confident now that the prize was inside her plaid.

"But you didnae," he said softly.

He knew better than to walk with her the long quiet track to Greenshaws. There would be other nights. He would put in an hour at the inn with the easy-virtued ale-wife there and go home later.

Molly made towards Greenshaws, stopping after quarter of a mile, only long enough to count out the promised fortune in gold sovereigns and quickly slide it back into the purse. She hurried on. She had never seen so much money before. She thought on Malky and smiled. He knew about the baby and didn't mind. It would be term day in three weeks. So after the two Sabbaths on the cutty stool to satisfy for her sin, she and Malky could get wed together and away, maybe to their own place ...

She hoped that the next girl at the farm wouldn't be so blate, or, if she was, that she would clash to the elders on Rob Lochrie of Greenshaws.

The Lady
in the Park

Edith Marsh walked in the park every day without fail and at almost exactly the same time ... as indeed she regulated everything else about her life. She knew the lime trees by the gate, the shrubs, the birds, the benches, the dogs and their owners, and where she would see squirrels. She knew it in every season, and this was the one she liked best. For this was late October and autumn had a pleasing melancholy about it that echoed her mood even more wryly than usual, the day before her fifty-sixth birthday.

She wasn't one for long country tramps in clumping thick brogues. Indeed from start to finish of her daily outing she could see the windows of her own west-end flat. There was a hedged railing round the park but Edith was tall enough to see over it and today she noticed the pleasing pattern made by the sunshine and bare branches against the honey, ashlar stone of her tenement block.

No, she wasn't a long trudger. Indeed no more than half-an-hour would have passed before her sensible brown shoes mounted the twenty-two steps up the tiled close, and she would hang up her felt hat with the feather in the side, on the hall-stand.

By then it would be quarter-past-four, tea-time. She had baked a few scones in the morning and would warm up one of those to have with her tea at the fire while she read her *Glasgow Herald*. The rest of the batch she would hand in later to the young couple across the landing, as she did twice a week. That, and a friendly word in passing, was the extent of her intimacy with them, for Edith was not only quarter of a century older, she was also out of her own time, old-fashioned, perhaps a little prim, compared with other middle-aged people she knew. Perhaps, she thought sometimes, because she had been the late, only child of middle-aged parents.

"Let your hair down, Marshy," the girls in the office had used to tease her, and she would smile, touch her fading chestnut bun and wonder whether, if she had loosened it, it would have shocked them to see it fall to her waist. Instead, she had laughingly chased them back to their typewriters.

She had been quite sorry to leave the office, but her old mother had become too confused to be left alone and, without murmur or repine, Edith had taken early retirement. She had enjoyed the farewell-cake one of the girls had baked, thanked the staff for the duvet they had clubbed together to buy for her, emptied her shelf in the staff cupboard, and gone. That duvet was the newest-fangled thing she had in the house and she had come to like it quite well.

Edith was alone now and, in spite of a niggle of guilt that it was so, was enjoying her freedom and the ordered routine she had established for herself. That daily walk at three forty-five, was part of the steady rhythm of her days. She rose at eight, prepared toast and marmalade, cereal and Earl Grey tea. By then the bed was aired, the duvet could be straightened and the bedspread drawn up (for she fancied the duvet alone made an untidy bed). She did each day's chores in unvarying sequence and finished the forenoon in Byres Road shopping for her few requirements. After lunch she indulged in the small pleasures of life, the watering of plants, changing of library books, the calls on one or other of her small circle of acquaintances, retired like herself, or widowed. There might be an hour or two in Sauchiehall Street, or a visit to one of the more traditional galleries. But whatever the early afternoon programme, unless the weather was impossible she was in the park by quarter-to-four. As she was now. Edith enjoyed the kind of reserved sociability she had with others in the park, the dog-walkers, girls pushing prams, young businessmen taking long-legged short-cuts between their cars and offices, students coming from classes. She knew some of them quite well by sight. There would be a smile, a murmur about the weather, but no responsibility to take matters further. Exactly as she liked it.

By this time of year when the weather grew sharper she began to wear a burberry over her tweed suit and carry in its pocket a bag of crumbs (the trimmings of her morning toast) to feed the birds.

Today, as always, she walked to the bench which was her turning point, and where a family of chaffinches fluttered, and pecked at seed heads. As she sat down, a gentleman rose from the bench, lifted a Glenurquhart cap briefly and walked off whisking away little flurries of autumn leaves at his feet with a walking-stick. Edith had nodded politely to the stranger. Now she took the bag of crumbs from her pocket, scattered them to the birds and looked forward to the National Trust lecture in the evening.

For the next three days, precisely the same scene was played out, then on the Thursday, he rose, lifted his cap as she reached the bench, and sat down again when she took her place.

"You're a bird-lover, Ma'am?"

Edith smiled and threw a spread of crumbs.

"It gets hard for them to find food in the winter."

"I've lived abroad where it's warm all year round and they don't have that problem."

"I expect they have others." She emptied the paper bag, folded it up and put it in her pocket. "Perhaps you find it cold here yourself," she said pleasantly.

"A little," he agreed.

She stood up, shook a crumb or two from her coat.

"Time to go back now. Enjoy your walk," she said and moved off, thinking of her newspaper and her tea by the fire.

He was there again on Tuesday and Wednesday of the next week. The 'warm country', it seemed, was Sri Lanka and he had retired home to settle down after twenty-seven years in 'tea'. On Friday he walked back with her to the gate. His name was Henry, and he called her 'Edith' which she thought a little presumptuous. But he was otherwise perfectly polite.

The following Monday he, too, brought crumbs and fed the chaffinches along with her. Midweek they went to see the plants in the park glass-house and, for the first time in five years, she missed her four o'clock tea with the *Herald*.

She was relieved when Thursday and Friday passed without her seeing Henry, then a little disappointed, and anxious, on Sunday. It had been a touch of 'flu, he told her on Monday... very commanding. His blue eyes did seem tired.

On Tuesday, she began to put on her coat at three o'clock instead of three-fifteen. He seemed always to be a little earlier in the park than she was. Then she chided herself and took it off again, sat down for ten minutes. She could hear her mother's voice from long ago, pointing out that eagerness was neither genteel nor modest. Not that she was eager. There was nothing to be eager about. He was simply a courteous man, of her own sort.

In November he had tickets for a concert in the City Hall. When she hesitated he assured her that he was using them for a friend. Edith knew that was a lie ... but it was a kind one.

She enjoyed the concert. Very much. But it left her with a problem of nicety. It nagged at her that evening after her meal as she put away her cutlery, her cup and saucer, and folded her tray-cloth into the kitchen drawer. And it nagged all evening as she sat sewing for the church Christmas sale, and even when she brushed her hair, lit her bedside lamp, slipped on her long-sleeved nightdress and climbed into bed. She could suggest a visit to the Art Gallery or take Henry as her guest to the Trust film next week. If she did, would that be forward? If she did not, would it be impolite after his kindness to her?

She didn't sleep as well as usual, but by morning had decided that, on the whole, it would be silly not to. They were, after all, only two rather elderly people who were not likely to upset their lives by spending a casual hour or two in each other's company.

And that was the security, that sense of her own measured routine being scarcely ruffled by her acquaintance with Henry, that wrapped Edith round over the next weeks as they went to Kelvingrove, the Hunterian Museum, the Fossil Grove, as she set his Christmas card on her mantelpiece, had tea with him at the Rennie Mackintosh Willow Room, and argued mildly about two ballets they had seen in the Theatre Royal.

It was in April that he asked her to marry him; as they sat under trees that were beginning to bead with spring green. The chaffinches pecked restlessly at their feed, fluttering, hopping away, coming back. Edith felt a clutch of something like regret somewhere below her chest, and wondered if he could see that she was trembling. She valued his friendship. But marriage! She thought of her neat bed and her small fastidious nightly routines, her bath, her hair, her slippers and comfortable old dressing-gown, the plain nightdress always laid out ready on her bed, the prayers, the ten minutes of reading, the flick of the lamp switch . . . and private sleep. If she could have shared those with any man it would have been someone like Henry with his sandy moustache and neat collars; and the polished shoes she was looking at just now. But it was all impossible to imagine. A man's pyjamas beside her own, a man coming out of her bathroom, padding about her bedroom, seeing her loosened hair, a man's head on the pillow beside hers, a man pulling up the duvet cover over them both — unthinkable!

"Does it take so much thought?" he asked gently.

"Henry, I'm sorry." Panic strangled her voice. "I just couldn't."

Henry had been tolerably sure she would say yes. If she had even said she would think about it . . . asked for longer to get to know him. Henry was hurt. '*Couldn't*' seemed like distaste for him and what he was offering.

"No, Henry, I couldn't." She was upset. "Please go away."

He rose, not knowing what else to do, or say, bowed a little stiffly, put on his cap and walked quickly along the straight path towards the gate.

Edith sat still, colder than ever now. Shivering. A young couple wandered past, the girl in a long flapping skirt and a yellow blouse hanging off one bare shoulder. The boy had his arm too far round her waist and was bending to kiss her. Edith turned her head discreetly. It would have been the same for her ... not in the park of course, she glanced up at her windows ... but there, in her own quiet home.

She settled her hat more firmly on her head and almost laughed at the vision, but the laugh was really a small sob and tears matched the onset of a drizzle of rain on her face. It would have been nice somehow to be Mrs. Frazer ... a wife. Dear, kind Henry ... she was going to miss him very much, for he would surely find another place to walk. Five months she had had of his company. Well, she had had nearly five years of the park before that, and enjoyed her solitary outings. Now she would enjoy them again. But the thought was as bleak as the years ahead.

She watched him growing smaller as he reached the far gate under the lime trees. Then she dabbed briskly at her nose with a handkerchief and told herself she was a foolish old woman. She saw him slow down, stand a moment then turn and walk back. He stood in front of her, both hands on the stick, his cap crushed between them.

"Could you try, Edith?"

There was a pause. Two or three people passed, nobody caring.

"I could try, Henry," she whispered, and rose to take his arm.

The Blue Spirit

The aborigine boy, Sakai, stood on an overhang of sandy earth which was held firm by soil-fast boulders and a mesh of tropical roots and ferns. A waterfall sang behind him and fell to a jungle pool where he had just bathed, and from that pool a second fall tipped over into a lower pool. Water glistened on the dark satin body, small-made and slim, and naked except for a faded blue cloth round his loins and a necklet of fruit-seeds round his throat. He tossed back the hair that hung to his shoulders, and lifted his butterfly net from the ground.

Born fourteen years before among the Mai Darat 'hill' people, who lived far off the road which spirals round the sloping contours of the mountain group forming the Cameron Highlands of Malaysia, Sakai's home was with an uncle whom he neither loved nor hated. The boy was as shy and wild as the butterflies he hunted, and as mute. He shunned the roadside and the haunts of men, his own tribal kind as well as the market-gardeners who grew cabbages on the terraces cut from the hillsides, and the tea-pickers who worked on plantations and plateaux cleared from the jungle. He felt closer to the creatures and plants of the forest than to men, and knew better than any of his people where to find them. He loved them all, especially the butterflies he took so gently with a smooth upward sweep of his net and slipped so carefully into the tin box slung at his side. It was bottomed with damp sand to keep the butterflies relaxed and not to harm the quivering jewelled wings. No other Darat boy or man could find as unerringly the great bright blue one that pleased his uncle so much.

Sakai's mother was long dead, but he could remember his

father. It had been that quiet walker in the jungle who had patiently shown him how to tempt one particular species to a bush by hanging a rotting pineapple or banana there, and taught him the names for all the moths and lace-wings by scratching the words with a stick on the ground. It had been his father who had shown him the haunts of all the creatures of the Highland and how to 'friend' them. But then he had died under a lightning-struck tree in a storm, along with the old mission priest, who had shared his love of the forest and taught him to make the letters giving names to what they saw.

Sakai was sometimes puzzled that his father's brother should feed and shelter him for doing no more than hunt butterflies and help maintain their attap-thatch hut, which sat deep among the ferns and undergrowth. But the others of his five-hut village knew why. They called him 'Sakai' (the slave), and his uncle 'Kikir' the greedy one. It was true that as long as there was daylight the boy was out of the way stalking the Golden Birdwing, the Chocolate Tiger, the little Dart, and the beautiful White Tree Nymph which fluttered tantalisingly high in the tree-tops. But years ago, when Sakai was not yet grown, Kikir had grumbled bitterly when he discovered the boy's distaste for killing squirrels and monkeys and small jungle rodents, hunting them with blow-pipe darts tipped with poison of the upas tree. He had struck Sakai when he had refused to hunt, but the boy had always obstinately stood his ground, turning away from eating trapped meat, and even releasing the bamboo snares when he found them.

Once he had threatened to desert the man and go to live with the crop raisers, but Kikir knew the boy's skill with the butterflies and with the gathering of wild honey that seemed to drop more freely into Sakai's coconut shell than any other, and signed to him angrily that he had better earn his keep with those, if he would not hunt.

It was then that his uncle had told him of the white man in a hut beside the road, higher up the mountain, who painted pictures of the butterflies and paid to have fresh ones every day to copy and then release safely back into the jungle. Sakai scarcely understood for he had rarely seen a white man, and never a painter of pictures, but for him to pass his time finding the creatures for such a man to admire, filled his days with pleasure.

He was a solitary wanderer in the forest, for the few others of his age in his village or on other slopes of the Highland, fearing that the deaf-mute was bewitched or not man-stuff at all, found courage in despising him for rejecting the poisonous white latex of the upas tree, but secretly wishing they had his skill with the butterflies.

The morning was rain-bright and soft and since sunrise he had been following the one he called the Blue Spirit . . . the one that was so rare. It had danced its way into reaches of the jungle unfamiliar to him, and then he had lost it. He had rested by the pool under the waterfall and swum there naked and cool. Now he stood on the ledge, still and waiting, to see if the butterfly had folded its wings on any of the greenery beside the running water.

A quiver of movement, a flutter of bright blue on a bracken by the second fall, alerted him and he crept forward lithe and soft-footed. The butterfly had spread its wings and flitted out of reach again but Sakai did not even see it go, for his petrified attention was held utterly by what he saw at the lower pool.

A girl of about his own age sat on a boulder there with her bare feet in the water. But he had never seen a girl like this before. She had hair the colour of sunshine and skin like the milk of coconut, and she was absorbed in watching the water lap over toe nails pink as blossom.

It was only then that he realised how perilously near the road his chase had brought him for, down below, he could see one of the motor-cars that he knew thundered past every day along with the lorries loaded from the vegetable farms. Usually a glimpse was enough to warn him to retreat deeper into the forest. But this car was at rest. It was the colour of the Red Flashwing he had in his tin and it sat in the shade of tall overhanging banana plants. It's roof was open and he could see two people lying back in it with their eyes closed.

Flight from the golden girl at the pool would have been easy enough but something stirred in him and held him there. The girl had raised her head now and was looking across the pool at a clump of green bamboo. His eyes followed her gaze and he saw the shimmer of the Blue Spirit on a frond of fern, and now, in the chance of his catch as well as his curiosity about the girl, he shed his fears. His footfall, usually so silent, cracked a twig. He did not hear, but he felt it, and thought the girl would run away. But only a momentary glance of disturbance flickered in the grey eyes she turned on him as she lifted her head. When she saw no threat in his bright, deep-set ones, she threw back the mane of silky hair, smiled, then put her finger to her lips as she pointed out the butterfly. There was a flash of white in Sakai's dark face and he smiled as he had not smiled since the day he had found the shattered bodies of his father and his friend the priest.

"Look, there! Isn't it beautiful? It has wings like velvet." Her lips moved and Sakai shook his head. She thought he could not speak her language and accepted him merely as of other speech and that to make each other understand they must make signs.

A warmth rose in him that she saw him as no more strange than that. He wanted to give her something in return, perhaps let her feel the gentle brush of the Blue Spirit on her hand. But in their moment of meeting it had fluttered swiftly out of sight.

He beckoned her. She pulled on her sandals and followed him, with only a quick glance back to make sure that her parents were still sleeping off their picnic. He led her deeper into the tangle of roots and lush green bush, past tattered banana branches and fern still wet with rain, and halted her in a clearing to watch three jet-black and green Rajah butterflies hovering round a clump of flower seed-heads. Then he parted a heavy curtain of liana creepers where the sun filtered in shafts on to a growth of wild hibiscus, and where, in a moment, black and tawny Batiks, with their filigree wings, appeared, alighting on the splaying shoots. Then the two moved on to a rise and a red soft-stone ledge from where they could look down on tree tops below and see the White Tree Nymph, blacktached and delicate. At another pool they saw scarlet, turquoise and golden dragonflies pricking the surface. She laughed softly and the delight in her face, as he showed her his treasures in those secret places, was her thanks for his gift of all he had of value in the world.

And yet he had not given quite all, for above everything now he wanted her to see again the Blue Spirit and feel the touch of it on her hand. He picked a blossom from the blue wild-pea creeper, held the cane of his net in his teeth and formed wings with his stubby, scarred fingers, frowned slightly and shook his head, and she knew without words that he meant them to find the blue butterfly again, but that it was not often to be seen.

For a moment their eyes met and they stood still. Because it would offend the gods if he should look at his reflection in the jungle pools, he was ignorant of his beauty . . . his fleet grace and dark oneness with this place. She was as fair as the Peace-rose of her cultivated world, but she forgot that now, and each was only intensely aware of awe, and brief joy in the other.

Then a shout, with a ring of alarm in it for the girl, came to them from far down at the road. The spell was broken and they knew now that they would not find the blue butterfly together.

The girl's lips moved and he knew she was saying 'thank you' and 'goodbye'. Wonderingly he put out a timid hand and touched her arm where the fair downy hair grew on it. Then he took the string of seeds from round his neck and put it round hers. It was not the Blue Spirit, but it was something. She hesitated then took his hand for him to lead her back along the path to the road again.

He left her there and watched her go. He looked at the rough hand which had held her smooth one, then turned and walked back into the forest.

His uncle had eaten and there was a plate of rice and vegetables on the mat for him. Kikir was impatient for him to finish, for from now on there was to be a new arrangement to their days, and twice he made to strike Sakai in his urgency for the boy to understand.

Several times recently the uncle had been on the road when motoring tourists had stopped and leapt out of their cars with their cameras, at the sight of such a man in his loincloth and out hunting with the deadly blow pipe. The white people had given him dollars just to stand for a moment and be photographed, and it seemed to the man that this was an easy way of making a fair addition to his living. When he was hunting he was seldom on the road except to cross it from the higher area of jungle to the lower; but if he were to lurk at the forest edges, waiting for the cars that wound their way up to the other world of hotels and golf courses, he might make his fortune. This very afternoon he would begin. He had always taken the butterflies from the boy to deliver them to Lim's hut, but Sakai himself would have to take them now, for they could not neglect that income. It was time, anyway, that the boy learned the truth about the trade there. He himself would collect the payment from Lim later. He would not trust Sakai to carry it home.

Sakai was puzzled at first over this change of routine, but his encounter of the morning had made him a little bolder about meeting the white painter of pictures.

On his way up past the Chinese township, where Kikir sometimes drank the whisky that stumbled his footsteps home, Sakai netted more butterflies than he could count on his fingers, to add to the ones he had taken in the morning. He supported his tin box carefully as he climbed past the market gardens where he had seldom ventured before, for fear of the tormenting children who lived there. But today he passed them without terror and at last found the butterfly hut.

Cautiously he peered through the window and in at the half-open door. Then he walked away again, afraid. But there was surely nothing to fear. He turned back, his feet moving silently.

But there was no white man there painting pictures and ready to free the butterflies when he had studied them. Instead a Chinese girl sat alone, surrounded by trays littered with the same variety of moths and butterflies that he had in his tin, but not so carefully carried, not such fine specimens. And, more than that, not moving. They were dead. There was no trace of that exquisite quiver that so delighted Sakai. The girl did not see him, she was bending over a cork strip balanced between a table and her lap and she was carefully pinning down the bright creatures one by one in a stiff little row. A bottle lay to one side of her and, as Sakai's horrified eyes took in the walls of the hut, he saw pictures hanging there with price tags on them, pictures surely, but not painted. Instead, ranged in rows, there were flat, cold glass-fronted boxes displaying, in all their glory, the frittering Lacewings, the Tigers, Wanderers, Nymphs and Birdwings. Dead. Even the great Blue Spirit was stretched motionless on a dry fern.

Sakai was mute, but he was not stupid. He knew that uncle of his, and understood that he had been deceived. He fled back down the mountain road and cut across the forest paths until he found himself near the two pools of the morning's meeting with the white girl. There he opened his box and emptied out the drowsing butterflies, sick at heart for the thousands of doomed creatures that over the years he had taken in his net.

Then through the great forest ferns he caught sight of the red car again, moving this time but still two road-bends away, and, remembering the glowing girl he had touched and loved in the morning, he ran to the jungle's edge and hid behind a tree to look at her once more. As the car passed, she saw him and waved excitedly from the window, holding up something to show him. Then the early joy of the day died in Sakai a second time, for one of the lovely rose-tipped fingers was pointing out triumphantly there, with the dried ferns and the Lacewings and Batiks, in one of the detestable glass boxes, the Blue Spirit butterfly pinned lifeless in the middle.

Davie Nicol's Obsessions

For a long time Davie Nicol, the cobbler in Largiedyke, had two secrets. One was a room; the other was its contents. Davie was a fifty-year-old bachelor, small, spare and weathered brown by sea-winds, who lived in that part of the Fife fishing village which curved closely round its busy harbour. The houses there then, were a cluster of red pantiles, crowsteps and jutting gables, oddly set as if they had been thrown haphazardly together so that some faced the sea, others shouldered their gables to it, and a few, reached by outside stairs, straddled two at ground level. And so in that jumble of homesteads it was not surprising that none of his friends noticed that, although Davie had three chimneys to his roof, they had only ever seen two rooms in his house, a bedroom and a back kitchen where he also kept his bench and last. In fact there was a tiny third apartment, up three or four steps from the level of the rest and entered by what his visitors had always taken to be simply the door of a hall press. Its window, half-hidden behind a chimney-pot, looked out over the lively waters of the Firth of Forth . . . although when Davie was busy in that room he never bothered to glance through it at the ever-changing scene of the fishing-boats sailing in and out round the harbour.

There may have been old people in Largiedyke who had known the house in their young days, but they were not of Davie's circle of friends and had probably in any case forgotten the rooms they had played in as children. Be that as it may,

Davie had been born in the house fifty years before, at the turn of the century, and, during his mother's widowed lifetime, visitors had been few and far between, and none so intimate that they had been peering into hall presses. Davie himself was quite a gregarious man, but nevertheless he relished the secret of his half-attic. And what the little room hid was the second secret the cobbler had ... or thought he had ... from friends and neighbours.

For Davie Nicol had a comparatively harmless vice, which was all mixed up with what psychiatrists twenty years later would have seen as his search for self-esteem, and also with a fear of being laughed at that he'd had since childhood. Nowadays it was probably about his unmarried status that he was most sensitive, but his private conviction that he had acquired something unique to himself, something special, gave him a real sense of compensation, a bulwark against those he suspected of laughing, however kindly, at him.

It was Davie's secret 'collection', housed in his secret attic, that gave him this satisfaction, a collection gathered over a period of some twenty years by the simple process of taking every opportunity of pocketing likeable small objects from wherever he happened to see them, (except from counters or shelves in stores, for there was a puritan streak in the cobbler which deterred him from actually shoplifting). But pubs, houses where he delivered boot repairs, even the homes of friends, were all rich fields for his pickings.

While no one suspected the existence of the museum chamber, most people in Largiedyke had a fair idea who was the magpie who removed their little knick-knacks. But those were hardworking folk, busy from dawn till gaslight and beyond, at the fishing or any of the dozen crafts supporting it, the nets, the coopering, the ropeworks, the oilskin-making, and so Davie's small knavery was worth only passing ribald comment. Besides, he was quite a likeable man who put his hand in his pocket readily enough in The Ship Tavern, or to put half-a-crown on a new baby's pillow.

"Just a bit siller for the bairn's guid health," he'd say and touch the petal cheek with a brown finger. Or he would dig a plot for a busy neighbour.

"The weeds grows quick, Joe Scobie, when you're awa' at the fishin'. I gie'd them a fork ower for you."

So, in spite of his sticky fingers, there were many who would still shake his hand and call him 'friend', although over the years they had learned to crack with him at the harbour wall or drink a dram with him in The Ship rather than have him home to high tea or supper as they had in earlier days. Even Lucy Ovenstone from the corner house never had him in now when her brothers were home from the fishing. But Davie knew she was working in the wool shop and simply concluded that she was too busy.

Davie's thefts were not for the gain they brought him, for the takings were rarely of much worth, nor were they of great practical use to him. They were purely for the pleasure of acquiring and squirrelling away in the little attic among the chimney pots where, after the kirk on a Sabbath morning and to the accompaniment of Salvation Army hymns played in the street below, he would spend a pleasant hour or two gloating over his pickings, whistling through his teeth and breaking off from time to time to murmur to himself about some piece he was especially fond of.

"A bonnie wee ashtray that ... what is't again? Ocht I ken, a PRESENT FAE DUNOON ... aye!"

He would handle them and re-arrange them as a man might admire and classify a collection of bird eggs or ancient coins. Among the dozens of trifles there were four paper knives, several briar pipes, strangely-marked shells, a tiny brass monkey, a Mauchline snuff-box, a barbolla-work pencil, a Diamond Jubilee caddy spoon, a sculpted cake of soap from the bathroom of a client, and one or two of the kind of travel books that, as a landlubber among bustling sea-going men, he found romantic.

At other hours, when he was out and about, Davie Nicol enjoyed the fresh air and sun, but when he was in his attic, perhaps for fear of prying eyes from other garrets, or even the beady stare of a passing seagull, he kept a tattered curtain dangling over the small window. That left the room even gloomier than its ancient brown paintwork made it already. But the treasures themselves glinted in thin shafts of sunlight and that was all that mattered to Davie.

And so for all the years of his bachelor prime, the little cobbler walked the waterfront of Largiedyke, bowed his head in the village kirk and delivered his repairs up the wynds and entries, hugging to himself at happy intervals the thought of the small room and the hoard of appealing gew-gaws there, known only to himself. His collection, he confidently expected, would grow, for stretching before him was an unending length of days in which to add variety and interest to his hobby. And never a thought had entered his head in half a century of robust good health that he could ever take to his bed, and certainly not with an illness that would offer the unlikelihood of ever leaving it alive.

But only a few days after he had added a prettily embroidered bookmark to his catalogue, for the first time in his life he was felled by a sudden fever. For twenty-four hours the symptoms were mild enough for his misery to be only that of any man heart-sorry for himself and wondering how he would endure the hours until he was recovered, but when he felt himself slipping in and out of consciousness and, at each small clawing back to sense, less and less able to lift head or hand, he knew he was dying. A terror of more than death took hold of him . . . the old mortification of hearing other 'dykers' laugh at him for being unwed, faded, and in its place came that of being uncovered as a common thief. For when the contents of the small room became known and friends identified all the things he had fondly imagined they had thought mislaid, his body would be lowered into the kirkyard, not with sadness and respect but amid sniggers and tongue-wagging.

Twice he left his bed and tried to struggle through the hallway to reach the attic and somehow burn or dispose of his hoard, but the short stair defeated him and he crawled groaning and exhausted back to bed.

Of course by the third day he was missed about Largiedyke and neighbours began to call. Lucy Ovenstone who played the tambourine in the Salvation Army band came first, on her way to a meeting at the Citadel. She heard him rambling wildly and quickly reported that Davie Nicol was in a bad way. After that they came in a steady trickle to pay what looked like being their second-last respects to the cobbler and talk in hushed tones about the old days.

"Aye man, I mind fine the time you pinched the teacher's sweeties and we a' hid in the jannie's glory-hole an' et them."

And in a lucid moment Davie smiled weakly and pondered on the long apprenticeship he'd served to his present folly.

At times he lay tossing, and at others so still and white that they thought he'd gone. But through it all he listened with dread that a set of footsteps would pause outside the hall press, that there would be a shocked silence and that within moments the bedroom would be full of angry voices or the much-feared laughter. And yet still there seemed to be no discovery, no fury, no mirth, and Davie would rest a little easier.

But death had not come for the cobbler yet and at last his fever broke.

"He's ta'en a turn for the better, has Davie Nicol," they were saying round the harbour. "Yon sunk look's off his jaws. He'll gie you a bit welcome noo when you put your face roon his door."

And so he did ... cautiously pleased to see Joe and Billy Scobie and Big Tam Ovenstone. But the most welcome face of all those that smiled round his bedroom door was that of Lucy Ovenstone, rosy, shining and wreathed in her Salvation bonnet. She said soothing prayers and held his hand and, since she was Martha as well as Mary, she brought flasks of hot milk, and nutty brown bread spread to the very crusts with fresh butter.

"Here y'are Davie Nicol. I'm come w'a bite to your tea." There would be scones or fruit loaf and small shepherd's pies with crisp golden furrows that made him feel better with every mouthful. Then on the two Sundays of his convalescence she was off to hallalujah with her tambourine and he lay back and enjoyed the sound of hymns floating up from the street. In fact, if it had not been for the nagging worry that someone would find his treasures, he would have been almost happy.

The day came at last when Davie's rubbery legs took his weight again and he was able to reach the attic, determined to make a start on getting rid of the filchings that had burdened his days of illness. He did not have the moral courage to return them to their owners. But keep them he could not.

He reached the top step of the short flight, opened the door, and gaped! The torn curtain was nowhere to be seen and, instead of the odd little pools of light on a general scene of gloom, sunshine flooded into the garret. Not only was every shelf and ledge bare of shells and snuff-boxes, beer-mats, candlesticks and PRESENTS FROM, but all was dusted and clean, and a jug of marigolds sat on the rickety table where he had handled and listed his prizes.

Davie went back to bed shaking, pulled the clothes over his head and waited for his due retribution. But two or three more days passed and no storm of abuse broke. Joe and Billy came with his newspapers, their wives plumped up his pillows and brushed his hearth, customers called with egg custards, and smiling Lucy Ovenstone cajoled him to sit up and eat the tempting suppers she had brought him.

In two more weeks Davie was himself again. The shanky gauntness filled out, the wan cheeks were whipped ruddy again as he went out into the sea winds. He was puzzled but heart-thankful to be rid of his collection, and cured forever of his obsession . . . though not without wayward pangs at the loss of them.

But there was another loss that was much more dismaying, for there was no need now for Lucy's visits and she was not one to make unseemly calls on a perfectly fit man. She nodded and smiled to him in the street as she had always done, then hurried on her way. And as she disappeared from view into a vennel or the doorway of the shop where she worked, Davie knew that he had a new obsession.

For two weeks he watched her coming down from the main street towards home and politely joined her to carry her basket to her front doorstep that had the marigolds growing beside it, and he even offered to go with her to her Army meeting. Lucy was not the woman to turn away the chance of seeing a soul saved, though if her tambourine ribbons flew wilder on those evenings, it was surely not only on account of Davie's soul.

They were married at Christmas among a crowd of hearty well-wishers, pleased for both of them. They moved into Davie's house, since Lucy decided that the little upstairs room, with a lick of sunshine yellow paint, a new carpet square and the comfortable chairs from her own home, would brighten up something wonderful as a sitting room where she and Davie could entertain. Their friends did visit ... in ones and twos, and they brought small gifts with them to hansel the new home. There were paper knives, a brass monkey, figurine mementos marked ARBROATH, ST. ANDREWS, and THE TROS-SACHS, a caddy-spoon engraved 1897. They handed them over sheepishly, but certain sure that Davie, at least, would like them.

The Dog and Duck

George Todd and Aristotle Whitakker had very little in common. True they were both thirtyish, lived in the same city street and worked for the same employer. But while George was still a bachelor supporting his mother on a small wage, and generally despondent about his hopes of winning the lady of his heart ... (Kitty Perkins who sang in the Wesleyan Chapel choir) Aristotle had been five years married and thought his Betsy lucky to have caught him. And although the two men lived in the same street, George's home with his mother was at the 'low end' in a one-down two-up brick terrace, while Aristotle was in one of the smart little bungalows at the 'up-end' with fancy drapes at the windows, a Georgian door with brass trims and Greek urns in the garden. Nor were they on a par at work for while George was simply a heaver-about of boxes at Mason's Furniture Warehouse, Aristotle was one of the company salesmen with a smooth tongue and flash clothes that charmed ladies into buying glass and chrome coffee-tables and macramé plant holders to dangle over them.

There were other differences also between the two men. The salesman was half-a-head taller and had a forty-four inch chest to George's thirty-eight; and while a small worry line, that George had had between his brows since timid boyhood, was now settling into etched permanency, Aristotle was handsome, hearty and brash, a winker-and-nudger who was the natural centre of attention wherever he went.

In short Aristotle Whitakker was a pain in the neck. It was partly his mother's fault. She had given him the Onassis name when it was in the news at the time of his birth, sure that she was beckoning fortune to her only boy. The same kind of considerations had attended all his rearing into the spoiled man he was now, a man who had to be cock-of-the-walk wherever he went.

He had certainly been one-up on poor George at every step of the way since they had been at school together, where he had sweet-talked teachers and come ahead of George in marks for all their subjects. At work it was the same. Both had started on the same day and after six months Aristotle was out of the crate-store and on to the sales floor and in two years a department manager with his own small staff. Aristotle had even whisked Betsy Connors from under the packer's nose and started courting her while George was still trying to pluck up courage to walk her home from work.

Their interests were different too. Aristotle's lay in cutting a dash at The Dog and Duck, especially on Ladies' Nights, and in taking trial drives in sporty cars he had no intention of buying. George's main pre-occupation, aside from yearning after Kitty of the Wesleyan choir (who had long, and more firmly, supplanted Betsy Connors in his affections) was hillwalking.

He lost his shy awkwardness and held everyone rapt in the pub when he talked about the sweeps and waters of the Tarn Dales. Then Aristotle would think enough attention had been paid to old George and cut across his account of leaping fish and wheatears, with some bawdy tale of his own, and if the crowd was still paying heed to George, and was not too numerous, he would order drinks all round and silence the hill-walker with a bored groan.

"Spare us the sparrowhawks and moor'en birds, George. There's a nest of fancier ones over there in the corner." And amid guffaws and giggles George would subside, and dwindle into his usual grey self again.

All the same it needled Aristotle to have to take a back seat on those occasions because there was this kind of kudos George had when he came back from a Saturday or Sunday on the hills and held the floor for a modest ten minutes. And when a burly delivery man from the brewery told the salesman one night to "belt up and let them hear George", Aristotle was ruffled. It didn't bear thinking about that the warehouse odd-jobber could get the better of him in the matter of tramping the hills.

"I'll come wi' you Saturday and see if there's owt t' them hills you're allus on about George. Right?" said Aristotle one night as they took the lane home to Mill Street from the pub.

George was good-natured. There was many a one he'd rather have had for company but, failing them, Aristotle Whitakker would do, to have with him when he explored Birtley Peak for the first time, that coming week-end. Besides he was a little flattered and had a sneaking hope that for once he would have something to show Aristotle.

When they met, George was wearing his old heathery pullover, ancient trousers, and boots that looked every inch of the several hundred miles of upland trudges on which they had served him. Aristotle wore a new green waxed cagoule, new corduroy breeches, smart heavy-tread climbing brogues, and sported a satchel that was natty with brass buckles and the latest in expanding straps. George had to acknowledge that he not only cut a fine figure in his outfit, but was well-equipped as well.

It was a crisp day of autumn sunshine when, after the train had taken them to a country halt, they set off on to the slopes. Aristotle with his longer stride outstripped George once or twice on the gentle approaches, and stood admiring russet ferns and brackens and urging on his companion as if he was flagging. But while the salesman was bumptious he was not stupid and when the going became a little tougher he quickly saw that George was hoarding the kind of reserves Aristotle himself would soon dissipate if he made too fast a pace. From time to time George pulled out a map and checked their position, a procedure which made Aristotle smile in these safe low foothills, thinking it over-cautious and namby-pamby. But George found landmarks and paths leading to other paths and ways through to the next stage of their tramp and Aristotle had to admit that he knew what he was about.

By early afternoon they were high enough to see part of the city in the distance and in another hour they found a ledge of rock and sat down to eat their food in sharpening but still clear air. They had long since passed the sprinkle of cottages on the lower reaches, although here and there around them sheep were grazing placidly and Aristotle began to feel some of the exhilaration that carried George away in the pub after such an outing.

"Aye, George lad, there's nowt like a day away from it all," he pronounced with satisfaction as if he and not George was the old hand at the hill-walking.

George only grunted. Not that the tang of the air and the sparkle and tumble of becks into cuts and gullies didn't exhilarate him, but because there was an ominous lowering of clouds over peaks some way to the north, and the thrust of the wind would bring it towards them before long.

As it turned out 'before long' was much more leeway than the two had, for George had scarcely begun to suggest that they had better be turning back when a mist came swirling out of the narrow valley to their right and half-hid the higher reaches of their path and, by the time they turned to seek its lower windings again, drifts of the mist were there too. Soon the way up was quite hidden and the track downwards visible only in tantalising glimpses.

This peak was unknown territory to George and the whole expedition a totally new experience for the bold Aristotle and when the mist suddenly banked thick all round them, they strayed off even the path at their feet as they tried to pick their way back step by step. Now they had lost all sense of direction and within quarter of an hour of the mist wrapping the hill they were hopelessly lost.

But this is not the story of how they stumbled and slipped and felt with their hands for the path, of their clutchings and wanderings nor yet, alas, of some brave and resourceful coup on George Todd's part to lead them both to safety, earning everlasting gratitude from Aristotle Whitakker. Because George was just as flummoxed and afraid as his companion. It is rather the tale of what happened when the two men were lucky enough to find their grasping hands working along the line of a low wall, to see the soft gleam of a light, and the contours of a small cottage looming at them out of the mist.

If Bethia Williams had come to work under him in 'Lounge and Soft Furnishings' she would have been entirely free of Aristotle's attentions behind the stock-room door, or if he had glanced at her on Ladies' Night at 'The Dog and Duck', he would not have looked twice unless it was to smirk at the shapeless tweed skirt, man's shirt and the unstyled hair. And if George had set her alongside Kitty, the Methodist lark, in *her* nice blue or green blouse with the pretty brooch at her neck, his good heart would have been sorry for her.

But alarmed at what might have been and chilled to the marrow, they both saw the plain, big-boned woman with the white teeth and warm brown eyes who served out bowlfuls of steaming soup to them from a black pot on the stove, as almost beautiful. And then they saw that those warm brown eyes were clouded a little and the woman could scarcely see more than the bulky shapes she moved between from stove to table.

George would have guessed her age as forty but Aristotle's experienced eyes told him she was probably several years younger, but worn and weathered by sun and storm.

The woman seemed shy at first but, truth to tell, (and she did tell, in all but words) she was a little hungry for men's company. Her attention to them was total as they sat with the smell on them of 'man', and damp wool drying.

"After me-Dad died, I'd nobbut t'do but g'on t'hill w'is sheep. There's never a soul wi'in six mile all round me 'ere and I'm in't town n'more'n two-three times i' the year."

As the men grew warmer and more relaxed George felt with gratifying pleasure that her disability set him for once on equal footing with Aristotle, but then the old, familiar underdog mantle fell on him as her working senses moved on and lingered finally, a little wistfully, on Aristotle.

The room was bare and shabby with two narrow armchairs and a sofa on checkered linoleum, and four bentwood chairs round a scrubbed table, but the stove-fire burned brightly and, beside a door which led through to the back quarters of the cottage, a grandfather clock ticked away, making a cheerful clunk on every other minute. She sensed them looking round at her few possessions.

"Me-Da put all't he had in't sheep," she explained.

When they had eaten she went to a cupboard and brought out a bottle.

"Made it meself," she told them as she opened it, put out three tumblers and sat on the sofa. "Juniper Dew, me-Da called it."

Whatever her Da called it, it had a kick like a mule and their first sip was but the start of a long evening. For a glance out of the window, before a sagging curtain was drawn, told them that they would be blanketed there in mist for the night.

"There's me-Da's sofa-bed here," said the woman, patting it to testify to its softness, and Aristotle moved over beside her to assure himself about its comfort, thinking as he did so that the more he looked at her the finer figure of a long-limbed lass did she become.

They talked of this and that, about their work and the sheep, about the way she could see light and dark, and shapes when the light was up or she was on the hill. They talked about the day's adventure, about Mill Street where the two men lived, of George's mother's terrace house, and of Aristotle's bungalow (though not a word of Mrs. Betsy Whitakker who lived there with him). There were times before midnight when in turn the men dozed off but they were all at least half-awake when the grandfather clock struck the witching hour, and the woman rose.

"Time for bed, lads. I got an early rise in't mornin'." And she felt for a travelling rug that had been folded across the back of the settee, showed them how to open out the bed and plumped up two cushions for pillows.

Then she went through the doorway to her own back room and, by the time George and Aristotle were under the rug on the sofa they could hear the sound of water running and the slap and lather of soap on skin, followed by a short silence and finally the creaking of bedsprings.

Of the two men George was the less used to passing a whole evening with a glass at his elbow and was asleep before Aristotle could get his mind properly off the woman through the wall who, in his rosying eyes, had progressed in the course of their acquaintance from gauche and lanky dowd to queenly creature of the wild.

The grandfather clock ticked and tocked an hour away. George snored beside him and Aristotle had the sensation of being the only being in that wide landscape who was still awake.

Then he heard the creak of the bedsprings again . . . and again, and knew that the woman was awake too, and restless. He lay very still, then heard a pillow being thumped.

He edged himself further from George, and paused. There was no sign of life from his bed-mate, so he put first one leg from under the cover then the other and turned silently on to the floor. George slept on. Aristotle padded through to the back room to see if he could bring a little comfort to the woman.

*

She was grateful after, and he knew it had been a long time, if indeed ever. She clung to him, told him that her name was Jess Ackroyd and shyly asked him his. Aristotle was not so overwhelmed that he was not still entirely the same fly salesman he was normally. He stroked her hair.

"George!" he answered her. "My name's 'George Todd'."

"'George'" she murmured, "'George Todd of Mill Street' . . . Got a good ring to't 'as that, George." And she drew him close again.

Aristotle preened himself as he came back before dawn and took up his prim position again on the sofa, alongside the sleeping George.

The next day came bright and tangy again as if the grey mists of the day before had never been. It seemed to George that the woman was more talkative to him this morning, even a little wary of Aristotle. Funny that.

But by ten o'clock none of it mattered, for by then Jess was out, high on the hill with the sheep and the two men well started on the tramp back down towards the low slopes and the fields they had to cross to reach the outskirts of the town, Aristotle repeatedly commenting on the comfortable sleep to be got, on even an old bed, after a hard day's hillwalking.

They did not have many more occasions, in the next nine months or so to talk over together the week-end adventure because Aristotle was seconded for almost all of that time to one of Mason's stores in the south-west and on his occasional week-ends home he supposed that, since he never happened to see George, he must be out tramping in the dales. George had done a little more hill-walking, although his experience of the sudden mist on Birtley Peak had kept him from further exploration there. But on the whole he had been pre-occupied with other matters.

When George and Aristotle did next meet it was one day when George was coming out of the Wesleyan Chapel in Mill Street. Aristotle was looking sleek and brave in a black leather jacket with cord lapels. He adopted the old 'success facing failure' stance as he folded his arms for a chat.

"George my son, how's things? What takes you in't t'chapel?"

George looked fittingly serious.

"Matter o' fact havin' a word wi' t'minister about my weddin'."

"You've been busy then since I saw you last. By-here George, don't reckon to've seen you since ... I don't rightly know when ..."

George remembered for him.

"The night t'mist cam' down on Birtley Peak. 'ave you mind o' that time, Aristotle?"

Aristotle had had a number of passing fancies during his exile in the south-west but he certainly did recall that outing.

"Aye I do that, George."

"An' you've mind o' the lass i' the cottage?"

"Aye," said Aristotle, suggesting a vagueness he did not feel.

147

"Seems more than nine months away now, but aye, it was October and this is July. Funny thing Aristotle ... I had a letter a week or two since, from a lawyer-man up Manchester ..."

A frisson passed over Aristotle and a flicker of images passed through his mind at those phrases of George's ... the lass in the cottage ... nine months ... the lawyer's letter. He saw the bare cottage bedroom on Birtley Peak, the brown dim-sighted eyes and hungry arms of Jess Ackroyd, he saw a picture of some straight-laced Manchester lawyer urging honour on the amorous hill-walker and remembered poor George coming out of the chapel after having to arrange a wedding. The frisson became a silent, inwardly convulsing chuckle at his own cautious shrewdness in giving her George's name.

'That's why,' thought Aristotle, 'that's why I'm a department manager and not but a packer of boxes and straw.'

"Aye, funny thing in't it Aristotle," George was going on, "but I'd've swore it was you she fancied that night, lad." Aristotle did not recall that George had ever called him 'lad' before. The warehouseman was still talking. "But it couldna been ... couldna been ... for she died o' her lungs there i' the spring. Sad that, in't it? Anyway she left me the lot. *The lot,* lad." George was not finished.

"Aye, a thousand or two from the house, no more'n that, but th'were jew'lry (George lingered over the word) ... and a' them sheep!"

And for the first time since they had met five minutes before, Aristotle really looked at George Todd. He was actually dapper. And the salesman had just a quick glimpse of a silk tie under his light jacket, when a rhythm of dainty heels clocked in small steps along the pavement, and George turned to take Kitty Perkins' neat blue-suited arm in his. He waved to Aristotle and moved off, the salesman going out of the packer's mind completely as he bent his head close to Kitty's to tell her about a grand little ranch-type house he'd seen out Dorrock way ... with tiled bathroom and all ... and that the minister would be happy to wed them on their chosen date.

Thaipusam

Ranga Ponnampulam could remember very few days in her life when her Mama and her Papa, her Grandmama and her Uncles had not spent all the hours from peep of day till dark malam, cooking rice and mee, and serving curry at the stall-restoran in front of their house. Sometimes one or other took a half day off, but tomorrow all of them would leave the rice-cooker and the frying pans, and the restoran would be shuttered for the whole day. For tomorrow was the start of Thaipusam. At eight years old Ranga knew that word as well as she knew her own name, because for forty-one days she had heard it and used it constantly and because there was a new frilly green dress hanging up ready for her to wear. Thaipusam came every year, of course, and some of the Uncles usually went, but this January was special because Uncle Mohan was going to walk in the procession from the big Hindu temple 'Sri Mahon Mariamman' in the city, out to Batu Caves. Then he was going to have a heavy kavadi lifted over him, a thousand curved needles hooked into his chest and back, and he was going to carry the kavadi and climb the two-hundred-and-seventy-two steps to the great cave-shrine, into the presence of the Lord Murugan.

"But why, Grandmama?"

And Grandmama would smile and hold Ranga close and tell her again that her Uncle was going in penitence for his sins and to ask from the Lord Murugan, in return, an easier life for them all. And then Grandmama would tell her the story of the Ancient Sage who had demanded two mountain peaks where he could meditate, and how Lord Murugan had flown up to the hills to find them. He never came back down and to this day those who go to plead at his feet have to climb high to worship him.

"And the kavadi? Tell about the kavadi . . ." Ranga would beg.

"The kavadi is like the chariot to carry the great Lord to the hill-top to be worshipped."

Uncle Mohan's kavadi was a semi-circular structure like the basket frames their neighbour made at his shop, but heavy, and with straps of wood arching down to a hoop at his waist level. A brace would be tied to his shoulders to take some of the weight and there would be a picture of Lord Murugan inside the kavadi. Grandmama and Mama had allowed Ranga to decorate the kavadi with paper flowers and peacock feathers, and with ribbons of yellow cloth wound in and out, all stitched with silver thread so that it truly glittered like a Sultan's carriage. All the neighbours had seen it and thought it magnificent and Uncle Mohan had allowed her to show it to her special school friends. She had felt important among the others that day, and had boldly stolen lollipops from the restoran jar to hand out to them all, after the showing of the kavadi.

And night after night Uncle Mohan would sit showing his friends the piece of paper with the design marked out on it where the hooks were to go in his back and chest, with silver chains hanging in a lacy pattern of loops. Then he would lower his voice and say something about the spears, and point over and over again to the same spots round his body and on his cheeks. Silver, his spears were, and he kept them wrapped carefully in the blanket he usually slept on. He didn't need the blanket just now because for forty nights he had slept on the bare floor and he had even kicked away his pillow.

"To make me stronger," he had told Ranga, and said the same about drinking only water and not eating anything at all. Which was funny because Mama and Grandmama were always telling her to 'eat up and get strong'.

Forty nights, and this was the last one. Ranga could not sleep for excitement. Tens of times she counted the planks in the wall opposite her mat, and tried to remember whether the loops were exactly the same on Uncle Mohan's back as on his chest. She got up once, found a pin and carefully pushed it through the top skin of her finger so that she could waggle it and the pin did not fall out. It wasn't sore at all really. He was very handsome, Uncle Mohan. All her friends said so, and he would look better tomorrow even than the picture of Lord Murugan himself. Then she thought perhaps it was wicked to think such thoughts. But he had such a straight nose and smooth dark cheeks and his hair curled all round his ears and neck. Then she slept and dreamed about the mountain peaks and the Sage, the cave and the spear, all in a jumble, with the people bowing down, not to Lord Murugan, but by mistake to Uncle Mohan, he was so handsome.

It was turning from dark to day when they all reached Mariamman Temple. Two white oxen were snorting and pawing the ground waiting to pull away the huge high silver chariot carrying the god's statue and the golden spear, that Grandmama had told in the story his mother had given him. Ranga could see jewels studding the great lord, and then there were so many people pushing and squeezing past each other that some of the time she could see nothing. A kind of moaning sigh rose from the crowd as the chariot rumbled off. There were priests and other important Temple men riding alongside, and people threw spices and rice. One of the important men sneezed and Ranga put her hand to her mouth and nearly laughed. Just behind Lord Murugan came women, singing verses from the holy Vedas, two other fat men, and then Uncle Mohan.

"He will be one of the first in the procession to Batu Caves because he registered early at the Temple," Papa said. Mama had given her some bananas on a wooden plate to take as a present for the god and Grandmama carried incense. Papa had brought two coconuts in a plastic bag. He cracked one on a stone, spilling the milk to pay tribute as the chariot passed, and two little boys pounced on the pieces and ran off with them.

There were drums and clashing cymbals, and a thin tune from a flute came piping out from all the beating. Uncle Mohan looked very fine in the loose yellow shirt Cik Darah had made for him on her sewing-machine. Some of the crowd closed in to follow the carriage, but Papa lifted her and pulled Mama and Grandmama clear of the rush. The other Uncles and the friend-uncles were already at Batu Caves with Uncle Mohan's kavadi and spears. It would be hours before the chariot reached there ... plenty of time to join the throng making for the 'Batu Caves Special' trains, and be out there before the procession.

At the caves they picknicked and watched stalls being set up. Banners fluttered, loudspeakers droned and the sun rose high and hot. Ranga fell asleep against her Mama's plump thigh and they woke her up when the chariot arrived with Lord Murugan and his golden spear.

"It is the symbol of might," her Papa told her learnedly. They were taken up ... up ... up, all those steps and into the cave. Then Papa carried her up too on his shoulder, and they saw them there, Lord Murugan and his sword. Then Papa broke his second coconut, Ranga left the bananas and they hurried down to watch for Uncle Mohan.

"Where is he now?"

"Half a mile back from the steps lah, at the holy river with the Uncles," Grandmama told her.

"The purifying and annointing," said Papa.

They began to hear drumbeats but there was no sign yet of Uncle Mohan. The drums and chanting grew louder. Sometimes it was "Vel, Vel, Vel!", and sometimes "Praise the Lord Murugan!" They bought her an ice-cream, a cold drink and a bead purse before the carriers began to come. Now and then through the crowd and the dust she caught glimpses of the first kavadis, twirling and swaying as the bearers danced to the rhythm, forward, back and sideways, forward, forward, turning all the time, over and over again. Ranga had never felt so proud. She was nearly choking with ecstasy. She pulled Papa's arm, jumping up and down.

"The peacock feathers, I see them, I see them!" And she broke from him and crept through a gap among skirts and trousers. One bottom after another she pushed aside until she was standing at the edge of a lane left clear for the kavadis coming. She looked up to smile to Uncle Mohan. But instead of *his* face what she saw was a dusty, dancing dervish, with Uncle Mohan's short spears thrust through his cheeks, and the other spears stuck right into him, all round his beautiful dark body. As he turned, the points of the spears swung round and the crowd drew back. These eyes were not the sparkling eyes of Uncle Mohan, they were glassy and staring, and the sweat was running down into them from his curly hair. His hands jerked on the kavadi and his bruised feet pounded the dust in time to the other Uncles' beating drums. It was just as if he couldn't help himself.

She would remember later exactly what she had seen. Indeed, she would never, all her life afterwards, forget it. Today she just stood there and tried to scream, but only a whimper came. Then she tried to run, but she could not lift her feet.

No one could make her speak when they found her. She clutched her purse and buried her head in Mama's lap. It was all black, black, black, and Uncle Mohan that she loved so much, must be a very bad man with terrible sins to have to do such a dreadful thing.

He came to see her in bed at night-time to show her that he was really alright and to bring her a lollipop. And then an even more terrible thought came, when she remembered stealing the lollipops for her friends. What if the family found out, and she had to push sharp things into her face to say she was sorry! Uncle Mohan came closer. He was holding the two ends of a stained yellow cloth to his face.

Next day they scolded her, and told her that people at the other end of the street had heard her scream.

A Kind of Awe

As he came through the house, Andrew Dalry heard the dull thud coming from his studio, and swore. Time and again he had insisted that the small extension where he worked should be left alone, not polished nor dusted with the fanatical zeal that his wife Rita applied to the rest of the house.

It had been neither dusting, nor polishing, not even tidying, that had brought about the thud, it had been Rita putting down one of her infernal floral arrangements on the table where Andrew had set a newly completed clay figure, ready for firing. A spray of greenery had caught it, tipped up the vase and sent the figure flying. When he opened the door he found Rita standing looking in some dismay at the head and two arms lying beside the dented stump of the figure he had called "Reaper".

Andrew was angry because Rita's dismay was rather less than he thought the tragedy deserved. He himself was sick with disappointment.

"Oh, I'm sorry Andrew. What a shame!"

"Why must you put that flower rubbish in here," he steamed. "That figure's been a week's work. The Aitkens are coming for it next week-end ... and you call it 'a shame'!"

Robert and Edith Aitken had bought a number of his figures now. He valued their judgement, for they bought as he worked, with artistic honesty ... not with an eye to spotting a winner or making an investment, but because they liked to possess beautiful things; water colours, small antiques, limited edition books. Andrew understood that and was happy to see his work part of the collection in their city home.

But Rita would not understand, and, although he raged on, he knew he was wasting his heat. His daily work might have been along the lane heaving sacks about in the grain-store bakehouse, for all her sensitivity to it.

"Come on Andy, don't get so het up. You can do another one, or repair that," she soothed, and began to gather up her bedraggled blooms, irritating him further. She mopped up spilt water with her apron and walked out of the studio humming.

Now Andrew was speechless, too furious to trust himself for the present with the fragments of his "Reaper". He lifted his anorak from a hook, took his sick heart out through the studio's side door, and tramped down towards the sea.

The Dalrys lived in the small town of Brandon on the island of Cormohr, off the west coast of Scotland. It was something of a compromise for them to live here, Andrew often thought. Life had an unhurried pace that suited his work and yet there was enough of the more social, trivial activities that suited Rita. Cormohr was within commuting distance of Glasgow for those who did not mind surly crossings in winter, an island of farmland, mountain and glen, of solid stone villas, bungalows, bijou converted cottages and a row or two of trimly-kept council houses. Brandon was its main settlement; on the whole a fairly prosperous community with two mini-markets, three unremarkable clothing stores, a chic boutique for the social set, a Chinese restaurant and, at the end of their own lane, a health food store which, as well as herbs and shop-baked grain-breads, sold organic vegetables, fresh flowers and half a dozen different kinds of local honey.

Beyond the boutique sat a small bookshop and gallery, where various artists and craftsmen, who had found the island a pleasant and peaceful place to work, held exhibitions. If they were lucky they sold their pieces to visitors, to discerning islanders and sometimes, as with the work of the more widely credited of the artists, to people who came to Cormohr to seek it out.

Andrew Dalry was one whose work was sought. He would

have readily admitted that he was not of the top flight of artists. He was not original, passionate, wild or visionary enough for that. But he had integrity, and never added a twist to his clay or a line to his wood carving that was not demanded by the direct pursuit of idea, movement or texture. Dalry's work was respected for having nothing about it of sentimentality or pander. The angled faces of his working countrymen and women reflected the often harsh, elemental demands of their labour and did not have about them the apple-cheeked joy in the rural scene wished on them by townspeople. His work was in demand in modest art circles, and, along with the twice-weekly evening class he taught at the island academy and Rita's pin-money job, it kept them in reasonable comfort in the small stone house, half-hidden along a wooded lane running back from the shore.

When Andrew had stormed out of the house his rage had not been only over the ruined work, it had been shot through and compounded by the same sour feeling he had had from time to time before, that he had married the wrong woman.

He had been young and foolish when he had done that, twenty-five years ago at the age of twenty-three, bewitched by a pretty face. And Rita with her fluffy hair and blue-grey eyes had certainly been captivating. She had been slim and vivacious and he had thought, as he had painted her then, that the fine bone structure of her face would give her classic good looks into old age. But her hair was faded now and her face had become plump, even pudgy, round the good bones.

As he emerged from the lane towards the foreshore he turned, savagely kicked a stone back into a blackthorn tree, then swung round again, hunched his shoulders to the wind off the shore, and strode along a path among the sand-dunes.

Disappointed though he was on his black days, that Rita had not preserved better, it was her lack of sympathy with his work, her lack of feeling, that was the ongoing soreness for him, a failing she had just displayed yet again. She was a thoroughly nice woman, conventional and suburban still, even after twenty years of island life; good-natured, generous and warm and, he supposed, quite tolerant with him. But she could not, or would not, share or comprehend the intensity of his desire to create things that would long outlast him. That was the nub of his resentment. He sometimes thought that his joy in the handling of a well-finished piece that would be an enduring testimony to his having lived, was a kind of triumphant compensation for having had no children. Rita's compensation (if she needed one, for she had never said so) was the part-time work she had as the doctor's receptionist, a regular coffee morning with friends and the local Flower Club whose meetings were the highlight of her week. Surely she had been more interesting than that in their courting days when he had hardly been able to wait to catch sight of her tripping lightly along the pavement to meet him and spend the evening in the park or picture-house.

There were days when none of this irked him at all, but there were others when it rankled that there was no meeting of minds between them. And this was surely one.

It was a grey day and the sea winds of late March whipped in across the shore and blew away something of his anger. He knew he could have his "Reaper" ready again in time, for he modelled quickly and would work on through the night if necessary, as he often did when he was afraid of losing the feel and rhythm of a piece. But the madness remained about Rita's shortcomings and he dug his hands deep into his pockets as he trudged gloomily along the sea-grass.

The dunes were five or six feet above the sand here and he could see three boys a little further along, playing on the otherwise deserted shore. He reached a broken-down bench and sat on it moodily to watch what they were doing. Two of the boys, perhaps about twelve years old, were hammering cheerfully at the planking of an old wrecked boat upturned halfway down the beach about forty yards away, engrossed, and doubtless relishing the prospect of joyful adventure when their work was done. Andrew felt no need to rouse himself to a warning of danger if they put out from shore, for the rowing-boat would never be seaworthy and would fill with water the

moment it was pushed into the shallows ... a waste of time ...
Not of Andrew's time certainly, but even so, he felt needled
that their efforts were to so little purpose.

The other boy was younger, no more than nine, with hair
blonde and spiky as barley. His bare feet were blue with cold,
and he was building a sand castle. But such a castle! It had four
corner turrets, on three of them flags made from scraps of
paper speared on sedge-grass. It had curtain walls, battle-
ments with a white limpet decorating each one, and razor
sheels to mark the arrow-slits. There was a moat and a
cardboard drawbridge, with ring-pulls threaded with strips of
sea-weed to raise and lower it. The boy's small blae hands
patted and carved, embellished and smoothed, while his
tongue licked chafed lips as he worked in total concentration,
never heeding the creeping tide at his heels.

Andrew's heart sank in dismay for the boy, that his master-
piece was to be lost at the very peak of its perfection (although
surely a child who could make such a castle should have the
sense to build it above the tide-line). He was about to call
down, but one of the older boys was shouting, his voice clear on
the wind.

"You'll get soaked ... told you you were too near the
water." The small boy turned quickly and saw that the last
wave had almost reached his feet before sliding back down the
sand and sinking into the glassy wetness with a sort of sigh.

"I'm coming. I've just this bit to finish." And he squared off
the last castellation and stuck a flag into the fourth turret.

Then when the douche of cold water from the next wave
washed his feet he screamed with shocked joy, jumped up
laughing, rescued his shoes and stood there, skinny arms
akimbo, while a third wave blunted the castle and another
destroyed it altogether, leaving only a mound, a scattering of
shells and a sodden oblong of cardboard.

"Told you!" yelled the other boy.

The child shrugged and danced across to join them, carrying the shoes and leaving his castle to ooze away gently into the
sand.

"What's the odds," he was calling as he went. "I'll do a better one tomorrow."

Not seeming to feel the snell wind, all three were working at the boat now. But Andrew felt it. He scooped the anorak hood over his head and set off to walk slowly back along the dune path. His anger had quite evaporated and, since there had been no anger in Rita, he knew that she would have re-done her flowers by now, she and the house would be welcoming and orderly and the kettle would be on for tea.

She would have enjoyed rearranging the flowers ... she was always happy working with flowers ... like the boy with the sand ... the 'doing', not the 'having done' ... for there would be nothing to show for their efforts tomorrow. Their creations gone. Funny ... he had never thought of Rita's twigs and S-lines and oasis as 'creations' before.

He lifted his head and looked about him, as he had not looked on his outward walk, at the waves rolling majestically in, shrugging and dashing themselves in exultant life against a line of rocks, then dying back shapeless into the sea. He saw a flight of oystercatchers arc up sobbing from the shore in a perfect chevron flash of swift movement, white on black. They wheeled, landed again out of pattern, the moment of beauty over.

From the green buckets outside the health food store he lifted two bunches of daffodils, passed the time of day more affably than usual with the nurseryman-baker who ran it; and walked up the lane, pausing here and there to cut wands of blackthorn and willow to go with the daffodils.

It must have been ten years since he had bought flowers on impulse for Rita before. Then it had been an expensive bouquet to salve his conscience over a woman he had met on an art pilgrimage he had made alone to Paris one spring. But this eighty pence-worth of daffodils for her to take pleasure in arranging, was not an apology, nor a forgiveness over the breakage. It was for a recognition of something deeper than that. A kind of awe.

The Nobleman

There was scarcely any trace left of a limp in the steady trudge of young Dickon Wain as he came along the path by the side of the River Wear, making for Marfield to the south-west of Durham. That was thanks to the nursing of the monks in the little infirmary at Coldingham where he had been taken after sore wounding in the Border skirmish against reivers from north of the Tweed. It had not been the kind of great battle that King Henry V was presently engaging in, in France, but the fighting had been brutal and bloody. After no more than thirty minutes, sixteen of the troop had been killed and Lord Croke, their commander lay dead beside them. Dickon himself was alive only because he had rolled himself and his shattered leg under a great bush and lain still.

The Scots dead and wounded had been carried off by their fellows after the battle, and the rest of Lord Croke's casualties slung across saddles, as the English left the field. And so, when the monks had come looking for them, only Dickon was still there beneath the thick branches of the thorn.

He had been seven weeks in their care and, since then, more than a month on the way to find his late master's brother (as instructed before the battle, in the event of the Captain's death). He must join Sir Hugh Croke's army, lately back from an expedition in France.

Dickon was now sixteen. His parents had been tenants of Lord Croke. His gentle mother had taught the boy his letters and his father had had clerking plans for him. But just as he was turning from child to lad, they had died of a pestilence, and Lord Croke had claimed him for a soldier. Now he too was dead, and the only ties Dickon now had apart from obedience to his last wishes, were the new ones he would take on with Sir Hugh Croke at Marfield, at the end of this long journey.

For the sheer joy of testing out his recovered leg, he kicked a stone down into the river below and listened for its cheerful splash. Then he bared his fair head and, taking a package out of his bonnet, sat down to a meal of bread and cheese, with ale from the jar at his belt. He was thoughtful as he ate. That 'sheer joy' he had felt in his moment of well-being, was not echoed in his anticipation of service with Sir Hugh. It was not only that he knew nothing of this new master and what manner of man he might be but, rather, that the Border wars had blunted the craving for adventure he had had when he first rode north as a virgin soldier. He had been sickened by the hacking down in battle of vigorous youths and men and, even more, by the exultation on the faces of those whirling their axes and thrusting their blades. And he hadn't much cared to see his own sturdy leg butchered by a single blow, and be drenched in the pain of it.

The days spent with the monks at Coldingham had been the pleasantest of his life since the loss of his parents. He had been bandaged and bathed into comfort, and cossetted with warmth and well-cooked meals served at scrupulously appointed hours. He had lain comfortable in bed, listening to the sound of plainsong and the murmur of prayer echoing through the stone walls of chapel and cloister. Later, as he healed, he had limped about the gardens watching the brothers hoe and tend and harvest their herbs. He had worn clean clothing and been allowed to read the precious volumes in the library and watch the copying of the Gospels by the fathers. He had enjoyed the peace and the quiet ordering of life, all of it seeming a long way from the smell of blood and sweat that was his own lot.

Dickon threw his last crumbs to a fluttering of birds, clapped his bonnet on the blonde head that was his legacy from Viking forebears, and scrambled to his feet to continue his journey.

He had met few people in the last two hours, but from a

stretch of woodland to his right there now emerged another figure. Dickon quickened his steps a little, hopeful of company for a mile or two. The stranger was a youth of about the same age, but taller and broader than Dickon and with a mop of hair the colour of the tiger-lilies in the Coldingham garden. He smiled from a friendly, freckled face, and spoke.

"Well met, traveller, where are you bound for this fine day?" and with one sweep of the willow-switch, he cut the head neatly off a tall thistle.

"I'm making to Marfield to present myself to Sir Hugh Croke, I'm Dickon Wain ... and yourself?"

"Barnaby Rydal's the name and I'm for Durham Priory ... for my sins," he added, glum for a brief moment.

"Your sins! You mean you're to confess some crime to the priests?"

Barnaby laughed, his blue eyes bright again.

"No, not that .. yet. I'm to join them there as a novice. My uncle's old, near to death ... he's my guardian ... and wants to see me settled. He's a scholar himself and can't think of a better life than counting the beads and slopping holy water."

"It's not what you'd have for yourself then, if you could choose? What life have you a fancy for?" asked Dickon.

"Oh, to go seek my fortune ... be a player maybe ... travel the world ... *live!*" And Barnaby swung an arm out across the view of hills and moorland before them.

"It seems we're both malcontents, then. Here am I, bound for a soldier, and I'd settle easy for a quieter life without the sword."

They walked on, speaking of other matters ... their childhood, their families, their likes and hates and their most recent days. Then Barnaby stopped suddenly and faced Dickon.

"Soldiering! That would do me. Does Sir Hugh Croke know you, excepting by name? Are you a stranger to him?"

"A stranger? Yes. I'm to present myself as from the service of his brother who died in the fighting."

Barnaby clapped Dickon's shoulder.

"No more do the monks know me! Have you any taste for

cloister life? It seems you found it pleasant enough, these past months. You read and write some, Dickon Wain?"

It was as easy as that. Neither lad had family behind him to make enquiries and neither party at the receiving end for novice or soldier knew either boy by sight. Dickon became Barnaby Rydal, Rydal become Dickon Wain and with an hour or two to exchange necessary information, each took on the identity and the future of the other.

At the village of Chester-le-Street the new soldier marched off, out of Dickon's ken ... out of this tale ... to cover himself with later glory in the French wars. The new cleric-to-be, scarcely knowing whether to rejoice at release from a distasteful career in arms, or to tremble at the enormity of offering himself falsely at Durham Monastery.

He reached the cluster of houses in the deep loop of the River Wear and looked up in awe at the Cathedral and Castle on the cliff high above, dark against a banner-blue sky. He drew a long breath as he mounted the steep path, and was relieved to find that two other youths, who had climbed up by another track, had reached the north port before him. One of them rang the bell and presently an elderly monk shuffled from the gate-house to open it to them.

"William of Stanhope!" one youth declared himself.

"John Mark of Sedgewater!" called out the other.

"Barnaby of Woodburn," announced Dickon, less-decidedly, but as his wayfaring friend had advised. He felt more comfortable with only a Christian name and a place he had borrowed, rather than adding the 'Rydal', which rang so false to his ear.

There were five novices altogether, received with Dickon that day. One was the son of a Hexham lawyer, one that of a Durham merchant; two had already been serving-boys at Mass in the Cathedral and one a pupil in the Song School there. Barnaby of Woodburn was the 'nephew' of the dying scholar-tenant Henry Rydal.

The first few days of instruction, of prayers, of acquainting themselves with the Priory precincts, with one another and with the various ranks among the monks, passed quickly. John Westhinton, who was Prior of Durham, was travelling between the daughter cells of the Cathedral and not present for the formal receiving of the youths as novices. That initiation pleased Dickon's sense of order, the ritual donning of dark wool cowl, scapular and tunic robe, and the prayers for them to live there as good Benedictines.

That ceremony was followed by the allocation of dormitory and refectory places and the rest of the standard clothing, and then, when the Prior returned, by the attaching of each novice to a seasoned monk who would be his mentor. Dickon was disappointed a little that his guide was to be an old shambling monk called Father Ambrose who worked in the refectory and would surely not be of much support to him.

He had been nervous of discovery at first but, as the days went by, he relaxed and began to enjoy the new experiences and the prospect of a secure future. There would be drawbacks, of course, but he had heard often of monks who had small homes and families tucked away in quiet places where they visited them when they could; and indeed of others who found that many a wench, local to a monastery, was bewitched by a holy man. But meantime it was enough that he had clothes, regular meals and a neat bed in his own cubicle that he learned to call his 'carrell'. That was in the recently-built dormitory with its rows of high windows letting in the sun. He enjoyed sitting at table too, with the old Ambrose serving out meals and making a humble little bow to each monk along with his platter. There, in the refectory, Dickon could let his mind wander freely while the Portion for the day was read aloud by the monk appointed. When he was supposed to be asleep at night he would finger his new sandals and socks, then sigh with pleasure as he drew up his blanket round his ears.

At first Dickon was so physically grateful, so alive to his good fortune, that he was always swiftest on his feet when the bell rang at midnight for Matins, ready smoothed down before anyone else, his new leather belt fastened round the robe that served for night-shirt as well as day-tunic. He would be in his place for the procession to chapel when the senior deacons, who each oversaw novices or young monks, were still trying to gather their flocks.

Between Matins and Prime there were four hours of sleep, then the wash at dawn at the water-pipe in the cloister, a breakfast of meal-bread and ale, Chapter Mass at nine, silence periods, private meditation, and monastery meetings where business was conducted and punishment meted out to transgressors. In the months of summer when he was given duties of delving in the garden Dickon revelled in it all. He was eager, and at ease with his mentor Ambrose (who was anyway not one from whom even the pig-boy would have flinched) and his deacon Father William, spoke well of him to the eagle-eyed Prior Westhinton. Dickon, however confident with other, lesser superiors, was greatly in awe of the Prior and had never yet faced him in conversation.

But, as the days became shorter and the weather worsened so that cold crept into the stone buildings, and winds gusted about the cliff-top site of the Priory and through the cloisters, the rigours of his old life faded from mind and nostalgia rosied memories. His hands grew chapped with kitchen work and swollen with cold from the milking of the goats in the bleak shed. Sleep was disturbed night after night so that they could rise to go and mumble prayers and try to sing through chattering teeth. And he found it hard to be obedient or attentive to the quavering Ambrose whose stint in the refectory, they said, had lasted twenty years. Then Dickon began to see his soldier days differently. There had been obedience to orders in skirmishes or pitched battle, but there had been spells between, with ball-games, contests of skill, exhilarating horse-play, among the young soldiers. There had been long evenings with carousing companions, quaffing great pitchers of ale, there had been the looting from laid-waste hamlets of small treasures to sell at nearby towns. After days of marching on empty stomachs they had had stolen lambs to roast, chickens to turn to succulence over camp-fires. And between campaigns in winter and rough weather, they had bedded down in Lord

Croke's Great Hall in the glow of warm braziers, often with engaging servant-girls to keep them company.

He had not seen here in the community, any evidence of those tales of monks with women waiting for them in the town. But there had been seven days of bread and water for three of the novices found doing no worse than fishing down in the river, and laughing with each other after evening prayers instead of being abed.

Here there were no nights of sleeping exposed to bitter winds or the risk of injury and death. But the life of the monastery had its own rigours. From Matins to Vespers and Compline, the days were ruled by chant and bell. And if he remained here they would go on like that throughout his life, which might stretch to seventy, or even eighty years like that of old Ambrose ... the days and hours would be the same for ever.

What in the beginning he had found orderly and supportive, now irked him and for the life of him he could not understand the peace in the faces of the monks as they padded quietly about their duties.

There were two activities which Dickon did bear patiently. In the library he sharpened pens, carried books and parchments and mixed the inks for illuminating the books, was even allowed to practise the lettering himself. In the wardrobe-room he helped to make small repairs to fine vestments worn by the higher clergy on special holy days, and to those garments from the foundation's earliest days, which were kept in the treasury museums. As he stitched those, Dickon dreamed of a day when he himself might be a powerful Prince of the Church and be rid of menial chores. For he had observed over the months that the monks who had the privilege of working among the manuscripts and archives or of caring for the gold thread and embroideries in the vestment chamber were also those who read well at mealtimes and sang out the lessons clearly, with most meaning ... those who had come home after a spell of study at Oxford College ... those who spoke out best in the Chapter meetings. If he was to stay here and yet avoid the worst of the chores he must excel in the correct ways. All in all it was best he stayed, for he had lost his chance with Sir Hugh Croke and had nowhere else to go.

Lord Croke had had plans for Dickon Wain. In time, if the master had lived, the young man would have been taken into his master's counsels, trained up for leadership in war or over his tenantry, for the boy had been intelligent, literate and of good presence. Those gifts Dickon now began to hone for his monastic career. In bed at night he silently repeated to himself passages from the Gospels, turning each phrase to bring out its full resonance and rhythm. When he was alone in the garden or on errands outside the Priory, he sang hymns and chants until each piece rang true, each word came out clear and dramatic. Before Chapter meetings he rehearsed searching questions and how to put them well ... but modestly. He studied the life of Cuthbert, the Saint of Durham who lay in his shrine behind the High Altar. He studied the books of law and the Church histories of Bede.

Twice Father Ambrose had put a veined hand on him and said the same words.

"You make those holy readings as if you truly mean them. That is good, Barnaby of Woodburn."

But Dickon cared much more for his Dean's approval, for Deacon William was an under-Prior and a man worth impressing. But soon it was not only those two who took note of him. The whole community began to be aware that they had with them a young scholar who could go far. They listened with pleasure at mealtime when he read the lesson, and when his was the voice that rang out in the Cathedral itself. In council they murmured approval of the question put with such becoming gravity for so young a man.

In Westhinton's absence on a visit to Oxford the Under-Prior encouraged and commended him. He was sent less often now to drag casks and hams about, with the cellarer, or to the laundry to rub and rinse and hang out the monks' undershirts to dry. He was more often with the books and treasures than with the goats.

And yet something troubled Dickon. Six of them had

arrived at the Priory that same day. The others had been careful enough over their duties ... and obedient, save for a frolic or two on the riverbank. But they had moved about awkwardly, ill-at-ease for a long time in their tunics and scapulars. They had stammered their way haltingly through readings and, except for the song-school boy, had made a poor showing in solo singing at Mass. And even that lad had sat dumb at Chapter sessions and looked up at Prior Westhinton with nervous smiles of ignorance, when questions were occasionally addressed to them.

Yet, one by one, those others had been called up before the Prior to hear reports on their progress from various supervisors, and then to be formally accepted into the next step of their novitiate. Of the six, only Dickon remained in the first stage. The only conceivable construction he could put on the matter was that he was already being groomed for a period of study at Oxford College. Perhaps that had been the Prior's recent business there. Whatever was afoot, Dickon set his teeth and, when Westhinton came back, continue to pursue excellence in the spheres that mattered.

Dickon grew skilled at the lettering and at laying out the pages of text. He knew the meanings of the designs on copes and mitres and on some of the Cathedral tapestries. He knew the history of the hill at Durham, the names of Kings and architects who had built on it, and of all the priors and superiors who had ruled there. But he was a little lonely now, for the companions of his green, high-spirited days at Durham had moved forward. Then there was also a puzzling round of work for him again in the vegetable garden and, while Father Ambrose was sick with the ague, in refectory and kitchen. In quiet times he paced the cloisters, wondering when he would hear of further studies at Oxford.

Sometimes he was sent to walk the three miles along the Wear to the small Finchale Priory, carrying books to the monks who, like Ambrose, were convalescent there from sickness. Or sometimes he attended one of those invalids, to or fro. On one such journey back to Durham, Father Ambrose was his companion, greatly failed now and fretting to get back to his refectory. As they walked the three miles the old man, staff in one hand, supported on the other side by Dickon's arm, whispered, almost incoherently, the Blessings, some of the Psalms and the Song of Charity. Dickon had to stifle impatience with the old man, because he had a new book with him for the library ... accounts of the lives of adventuring Christians. If they were quick he would have half-an-hour with it before High Mass.

Then, within sight of the north gate, Ambrose seemed to stumble. He fell, and Dickon knew, even before he could fold his scapular for a pillow, that the old monk was dead.

At the special service next day, the Prior spoke movingly and at length, of Father Ambrose's years of service to the Community, latterly for many years as food servitor. Dickon was but half-listening as the litany of the old man's virtues was recited, "holy, cheerful, humble, setting himself at naught in sweet obedience to God's will, a noble man." Dickon supposed the old monk had been worthy enough, but this was surely the poetry of requiem; for what else could such a man have done with his life in exchange for shelter and companionship. Westhinton was still speaking, Dickon's attention was caught and he looked up and met the eyes of the Prior ...

"A noble man ... of the Blood Royal, a prince in the counsels of his earthly King, a man of wealth and renown, who came in the prime of life, at the height of his fame, asking only to serve his Lord in the Benedictine order at Durham ... of such," said the Prior, "is the Kingdom of Heaven."

The choir sang until the soaring pillars echoed, the last words of the service were spoken, the procession around mitre, crozier and censer left the sanctuary. Dickon went towards the cloister, to go to his duties which today were with the cellarer. But his step was slow, for he thought, not of the work in the store, nor of the waste of his talents there, but of Father Ambrose ... and of the burden he himself had carried without recognition for a long time. Then he was aware that Prior Westhinton was at his side.

"Barnaby of Woodburn ... walk with me ten minutes in the cloister."

Suddenly Dickon found himself ready to deny the title.

"Father-Prior, every day since I came to Durham I have been in the confessional. But there is a lie I have carried that I have never spoken of."

"That you are not Barnaby of Woodburn."

"You know."

"I have known from the first day that I saw you. When I came home after your arrival I looked for the red-plumed lad written of by Henry Rydal when he sought a place for his nephew. Instead I found a yellow-haired young man, dragging his leg a little from a battle-wound ... just the kind of boy they told me in Coldingham they had recently nursed in their infirmary."

"My lord, you did not say!"

"You had been received. Perhaps you had a true vocation. There would be no harm done to wait and see. I waited."

"I did my work well. I pleased Deacon William and I read and sang to Father Ambrose's satisfaction."

"Ah, Father Ambrose ... God rest that great soul ... I made him your mentor ... that was not chance."

"I studied and I sought knowledge."

"But never, until today in the chapel, did you raise your eyes to look into my face. I have learned much of you ... whoever you are by true name."

"Richard ... 'Dickon'. I was born in Morpeth, Richard Wain."

"Richard then ... of Morpeth. I have seen that you are skilled and take pleasure in reading and in scripting, in singing hymns and raising prayers ... but that you do other work with a less cheerful heart, as though it were less exalted. But today I have seen something new, a kind of courage. That is what I have learned of you. What have you learned of us?"

Dickon was slow in reply. He had to think as he spoke, for he was confessing.

"I came here to escape the discipline and hardship of

fighting and being under harsh orders in battle ... to find shelter and food and an easier life."

"And what did you find?"

"That the discipline of the monk is harder than the soldier's because it is not just for the times of battle and training, but day after day, hour after hour, for life. That is harder."

"And did you find God, Richard of Morpeth?"

Dickon considered that, then spoke in sudden, shaken understanding.

"I did not even look for Him."

"Not in kitchen, or almshouse, or granary?"

"Not even in the Holy Books. I have found nothing."

"You have found honesty," said Westhinton quietly.

They started on another round of the cloisters.

"Now, you would leave us?"

"I had no true vocation when I came, but now I wish that I could stay and seek."

"That is all that we require of any man here."

For a moment Dickon had a glimpse of being received today ... at this moment ... as the others had been, his future, after all, among the books and gilded letters. But Prior Westhinton still spoke.

"... you must go back. See the two men you have wronged, Sir Hugh Croke, and Henry Rydal who is dying. Then you must spend a year in the world to find where your calling lies. Perhaps Sir Hugh will still offer you service with him. But if you come back to share our labours here, you will start again, with the vegetables and the goats and the scrubbing. Perhaps by then, there will be some here more skilled than you at the things in which you take pride now. You may find yourself like the good Ambrose, forever in refectory or farm," the Prior paused, suddenly, remembering. "Long ago, Dickon Wain, I myself was his body-servant and arms-bearer. All my life he has been my superior ... Now go away ... consider and meditate whether you are able to find such a man as you knew here, to be greater by far than yourself."

The bell rang for Vespers. The Prior put a hand of blessing

on the novice's shoulder, and was gone. Dickon turned away from the call to chapel, slowly mounted the steps to his carrell in the dormitory. There he removed cowl and scapular, and went to claim back his own clothing from the aumory.

No one but the janitor saw him go. He passed down the slope and over the bridge. Perhaps a year from now he would be enduring the hardships of life on a Border campaign or in some foreign war. Perhaps he would be back here ringing the north port bell seeking entry to an even more rigorous life, this time as Richard of Morpeth. Maybe, no matter which, he would be a better man.

The Grey Tin Plate

It was a mystery to young Annie MacBain how her mother could hate the old man so much; how she could push him out of her way when she was scrubbing the floor or shout at him for asking the same questions over and over again. Annie had never really thought how she felt about her mother. Her mother was just there, stirring things in pots, grunting over a washing-board, red in the face through clouds of steam from the clothes-boiler, or getting ready for her father and four great brothers who would be coming back after their shifts at the pit, needing hot water and big dinners. Her mother didn't shout at her or push her about. She wasn't cruel. No, Annie got her breakfast bread-and-dripping, and pancakes for tea, and on cold mornings her mother would pin her into a big crossed-over muffler ready for the walk to school. But her Ma wouldn't be looking at her because, at the same time, she would be seeing that the old man's brose wasn't burning, then giving it to him in the kitchen bed, and muttering that she'd more to do than run after a lazy old fool who couldn't get up in the morning and get out of her way to stand at the corner or go to the Public Library.

For most of the older men in Midton, the mining village strung out bleakly halfway along the main Glasgow-Edinburgh road, there wasn't much else, between the wars, but the corner and the reading room.

In spite of the pancakes and the warm muffler Annie wasn't a bit sure that she actually loved her mother, but she had no doubt at all that she loved her grandfather ... loved him so much that sometimes she woke whimpering in the night at the thought that someone so very old would surely die soon and leave her.

Annie was eight at that time and Daniel Drysdale sixty-nine and far from dying. He was a short stocky man who had spent his entire working life in the open air as a roadman. His skin was brown and weathered as autumn leaf and his heart and lungs in good fettle for a man touching seventy.

Daniel himself sometimes wondered if that's what it was that irked his daughter-in-law, that he had spent his life in God's good wind and sun, while her own menfolk were grey and had hard, sore coal coughs from living half their days like moles underground. Or maybe it was just that he was getting slow and was another mouth to feed, an extra bed to change, a sixth pair of long-johns to wash.

That Saturday he and Annie were taking their afternoon walk across the field path to the old quarry.

"She doesnae smile, Ma, sure she doesnae, Gran'pa?"

"Maybe she hasnae that much to smile aboot, hen. She's a hard life, y'ken. A' they women that's got men doon the pit has a hard life."

All the same, few of them were as humourless as Kate, Daniel thought, wincing at the memory of having slittered his soup on the table-cloth then, trying to rescue the bowl, skiting it off the table, smashing it against the range. He could still feel the slam of the door behind them as they left the two-room-and kitchen cottage in the old miners' row, and hear the angry shout that came from the other side.

"Get oot my sicht the both of yous."

Maybe if Kate used a nice bit oilcloth on the table like his Mary had done, and did not try so hard to be genteel, she wouldn't get into such a fash about a spill of broth. Pity about the bowl, mind.

But it was a fine May day and Annie and her grandfather had the whole afternoon together. She skipped along the path beside him, plump and pigtailed ... together till tea-time. Sometimes it was the river they went to on Saturdays. They saw the big flag iris there and the shoals of baggy minnies that wriggled away in huge families when her gran'pa swirled the water with his stick. There were monkey flowers there too, and sometimes a jerky little coot poking in and out of the riverbank. Her gran'pa knew where to find all these flowers and creatures and made her remember their names.

"Mind that wee flower's cried an 'eyebright', Annie hen."

"I cannae see a flower there at a'. It's just wee spear-things."

But they got down on their hunkers close to the patch of spears and he showed her the pinpoint flower.

"As blue as your ain eyes, pet."

Last summer too, they had seen raggy-robins, and the ladies' bedstraws that he made her look right into, to see the tiny cross that was each petal. Even on frosty winter days there were berries and the silver curls he called 'old man's beard'.

"Just like mine's," Gran'pa would say and they would laugh because his was short and bristly and still brown. On winter nights too, at the back door, he pointed out the stars. The Great Bear and The Plough, while her mother complained about the draught.

Gran'pa still had friends among the roadmen too. Sometimes they worked on the dry dyking and Annie liked to see how they tilted and balanced one stone on another with no mud to stick them together, but just right ... big stones with wee slivers tucked into the gaps. And never a one tumbled, even when she pushed them. Ernie and Coll knew about the flowers and trees too, and once they let her hold a field mouse in her own hand.

Today, on their way back from the quarry they saw them sitting at the roadside.

"We'll see them knappin' the stones the day."

"What's knappin'?" asked Annie.

"Weel the farmers doesnae like big stones in their fields so they carts them to the road and leaves them in a pile. Then the roadmen knaps them. You'll see."

Ernie and Coll sat on the hedgerow bank, a fat man and a thin man, eating their pieces and throwing crumbs to the chilfies that fluttered round their feet.

"Day t'you, Daniel, and you, hen. Are you keepin' him in order an' oot you Ma's road?"

That was so true that neither of them replied. The two men had wee heavy hammers to work the·stones.

"Why d'you sometimes just tap and other times gie them a right clout?"

"Och it's just the knack to get them a' the same size to put on the road."

Daniel clashed for maybe another quarter-hour with Ernie and Coll while Annie played with some of the chuckies. But there was still their other Saturday visit to make on their way home, once they were past the marsh pond. They knew better than take jars of spawn home, since the time last year, of the frogs jumping about the kitchen floor. But they liked the path by the pond.

"We're gettin' wir feet muddy, Gran-pa."

"Never heed that, hen. Look here at they wee taddies wi' their legs comin'.

The last stop on Saturdays was always Toni Capaldi's ice-cream hut. Daniel didn't fancy the ice-cream along with the taste of his wad of Bogey-roll, but for Annie he favoured a good big cone doused with raspberry.

And so the two cronies arrived on Kate's newly pipe-clayed door-slab, to break her heart with mud on their boots and dripping raspberry everywhere.

"My back's cut in two wi' the time I've put in on that step the day," she stormed. "An' now look at it ... and what are you fillin' the wean up wi' ice-cream for anyway, when your teas is on the table."

So it was. It was kippers and a pile of her Mother's Saturday scones and the table set with blue and white dishes for everyone ... except Daniel. His kipper went on the deep, grey enamel plate that usually covered left-overs in the press.

"You'll be best wi' that, Faither, it'll no' break." Annie's father and brothers were in now and there was a babble of crack and guffaw as they looked on. Annie was silent, hating her mother. She didn't know why really. It was right enough, her Gran'pa was clumsy and broke things sometimes, but she'd never liked that grey tin dish and the sound of his knife scraping on it now, making a different sound from eveyrone else's, was all wrong. It made him seem small, and not special, the way he really was ... *them* with their football and not one of them knowing a chilfie from a speug or The Seven Sisters from The Plough. For Annie the noise of her beloved grandfather's cutlery on that plate drowned out every other sound.

*

She had to endure it for seven more years before the day came when she sat in the darkened kitchen, fifteen years old now, but holding a wally scottie the old man had won for her once at the shows, and trying not to look at his coffin beside the bed. Annie had scarcely ever heard a kind word from her mother either *about* Daniel or *to* him, but now she saw Kate sniffing and dabbing at her nose with a handkerchief, and she wondered.

"I wasnae that kind to him," said her mother, as she and Annie were washing up later. "He was a good enough old chap." Annie didn't know what to say.

"You washed for'm and gie'd him good meat and a clean bed," was all she could think of, as she piled the dried plates on top of the grey tin one on the shelf.

"Aye, so I did," and Kate wrung out the dish-towel and threw it over the flowering-currant beside the kitchen door.

A knapper, who lived above ground and knew windflower from wild strawberry, might have suited Annie better, but in the end she married a collier and went to one of the new council houses in the centre of the village. Her man, Gib Rae, was no better or worse than any other and her lot not much different from that of any of her friends, not as unremitting as their mothers' but bedevilled by slump and short time. They washed and scrubbed, knitted jerseys for their men, and made-over skirts into trousers for their bairns. Annie was different only in that, when she took the back path to her mother's house, she could name to herself every plant and tree she passed and half-a-dozen of the butterflies that flittered about the clumps of thistle. That little ritual never failed to brighten her day.

By the time the war years were past, two of Annie's own three sons were down the pit with their father, one of her brothers had died at Dunkirk, one had been killed in a coal-face fall, a third had gone south to work and the youngest was doing wonders in America. Her father lay beside old Daniel in the cemetery. Her mother, Kate, was alone and wracked with the rheumatics, and now the colliery people needed the cottage in the Row ... Annie suggested having her mother to stay.

"She can come for a' I care, Annie. She's *your* Ma," said Gib casually. "You'll just hae to squeeze the housekeepin' a bit thinner."

Annie's youngest, Joe, was ten when Kate came to live with them. Annie was a placid woman. She ran a comfortable home, without being so houseproud as her mother, but with a regular routine, and she had no doubt at all that Granny, who had mellowed over the years, would fit in with that, without being too much of a nuisance. Her own easy-going nature would surfle out any rucks ... besides, young Joe, bright, spindly and pleasantly ugly, was the apple of both women's eyes. Annie had had more time with Joe than with her other children and she had tried to pass on some of old Daniel's lore of field and sky to the boy. Joe enjoyed being out-of-doors, but preferred kicking a ball with his friends to identifying birds or watching for shooting stars.

It was shortly after Annie's mother came, while Joe was at home from school nursing a football knee, that his grandmother first showed him how to bake scones. When Annie came in that day from the Co-op, where she worked three afternoons a week, she laughed at them and cheerfully swept the kitchen floor for the second time that day. Kate was tired. The next day it was pancakes, then flapjacks and potato scones and, before the convalescence was over, he was turning out soups and stews and pan haggis.

It wasn't just that Annie's routine of having the kitchen

reasonably fettled up each day by about one o'clock, was broken and she was left with spoons and bowls and vegetable peelings to clear up. No, it wasn't just that. She found it vaguely distasteful to see her son skiddling about like a lassie in the kitchen. And when he began to bring home cookery books from the library and pore over them with his grandmother, then there were angry words.

"You're makin' a right sissy i' that boy," accused Annie.

"Dinnae be daft, woman, where is he the noo? He's oot wi' Kevin and Sanny playin' football. Me learnin' him to cook and make a bit tattie scone's no' goin' to make a sissy i' a laddie like Joe."

"It's no' just that. It's my kitchen. Och, you were great guns on keepin' your own place perjinkety, but it doesnae matter if you leave mine's like a midden."

"Yours!" scoffed Kate. "You dinnae ken what a tidy kitchen looks like. There's nothin' I do that makes it worse."

After that, other irritations that Annie had ignored before, began to rankle. Her mother needled at Gib and made dark remarks to Annie behind his back. Some of them were true enough, but none of her mother's business. And there was the way Kate sat at the window and could see exactly where Annie went ... whether she turned in or out of the village or went straight across to her friend Sandra's. Then there was how she used both bars of the electric instead of an extra jersey on cool days. She changed her clothes and had baths twice a week ... twice! When a weekly wash-down had served her well enough in the Row ... and she left her teeth at night in a tumbler in the bathroom. But worst of all, she encouraged Joe in this fad of cooking and cutting out recipes. *And* she began to get wandered.

Annie could feel herself getting sour and crabbit over the pinpricks and she knew that she was deaving Sandra with her problems every time they met.

"Och, never heed her, Annie. She's just a selfish old woman," sympathised Sandra.

But that wasn't true and Annie didn't like it.

"No, no. She's no *just* a selfish old woman, Sandra. She's a lot of other things forbye that. She's good-natured right enough. She's fond of us, in her own way, and she'd gie us her last ha'penny."

All the same she felt stabs of jealousy when she noticed Joe beginning to greet Kate first when he came in from school. Other two of her mother's sins as she grew older were to put too much sugar in her tea then flett it, and drink it from the saucer. Annie tightened her lips and bore that for a week or two and then retaliated by setting the table with only the saucer at Kate's place ... no cup. She poured her mother's tea straight into it. There was a laugh from Gib and a coarse remark from one of the older boys. But it was Joe's silence that spoke loudest in Annie's ears, and when she caught the look in her son's eyes she recognised it, and remembered the grey tin plate. Joe went to the kitchen, brought a clean cup and saucer and set it before his grandmother.

Kate lived long enough to see Joe leave school at fifteen and get a job in the kitchen of The Plum Tree Roadhouse, six miles away. Then she failed quickly and took to bed and, although Annie surrounded her with rugs and hot water bottles, and scolded her to drink her hot milk, she took pneumonia and, in the end, died without a struggle.

The earth was not settled on the mound of her mother's grave before Annie was hard put to it to remember why they had lived at arm's length from each other for six years, with scarcely a warm word between them. Then her natural calm sough reasserted itself and the feeling of guilt and regret gave way to one of being like a bird set free from a cage. Only when Joe opened his first tiny restaurant outside Edinburgh eight years later and called it 'Kate's Corner' did the old resentment come briefly back. It did not last. She and Gib, in their sixties now and alone in the house, took a second notion to each other and enjoyed a year or two of jaunts to be special guests at 'Kate's Corner' and watch with awe as their youngest gravely served the plat du jour and checked that his toff clients were satisfied.

"Enjoy your meal, sir?"

Annie was perversely pleased that he behaved exactly the same way to plainer couples like themselves obviously on a rare night out.

Annie was a widow by the time Joe moved into what Gib would have called his 'posh place' in Edinburgh New Town and was ready to employ three or four waiters. He was married to an elegant, willowy girl who had been to George Watson's school and was not only a decorative presence in his restaurant but had gifts for choosing table appointments, buying well at the early markets and keeping exemplary books. She was so valuable to Joe there that it seemed a sensible idea for Annie, who was lonely now at Midton, to go and live with them in their pleasant new home out Balerno way, to be the kind of housekeeping presence there that would prevent their home being no more than a luxurious night shelter. Annie hesitated, remembering her own mother and her grandfather. But when she saw the garden, the burn running past and the green meadow beyond, and thought of walking there in the season-by-season changes, perhaps later with the grandchild soon to be born, she paid her last rent at Midton and packed up.

Her friend Sandra wondered briefly if she was sure.

"It'll no' be the same, Sandra. Joe's Susan's a right nice lassie and anyways she'll be back to the rest'urant in a wee while. We'll no' be tumblin' over each other. That's what was wrong before. Besides I'll no' interfere. I mind too well the things no' to say or do." She laughed. "I dinnae flett my tea y'ken."

"You'll be a model, then, eh?"

"Aye, somethin' like that."

And so she was at first. But, by the time young Alison was beginning to speak, Annie was certainly not the model Susan wanted for her daughter. There was a second new baby now and Susan had decided to hand over her work at the restaurant to a bright young assistant manager. Alison was delighted with her small brother and hung over the pram.

"You'll smother the baby if you hug him like that," protested Susan.

"No I'll no'. He's no' that wee!"

"Don't speak like that, Alison!" her mother said sharply, and corrected her word by word. Annie went into the kitchen, rebuked.

Over the next few weeks offending words like 'pieces' and 'tatties' and 'tumshies' were ironed out of the little girl's vocabulary, and dropped letters picked up. Tea was not 'masked' any more, and certainly not in the forenoon when it was 'coffee' anyway. Annie hated coffee, but she sipped it doggedly and tried to mind her Ps and Qs. She went walking nearly every day along the burn path, especially when Susan had friends in; because the first time that had happened she hadn't put a cup and saucer on the lounge trolley for her mother-in-law, and Annie had taken the hint. Well, that was right enough. They *were* her friends after all.

Annie did try, but she had off days: like when she put marsh marigolds on the mahogany table and the bottom of the jug had been wet and left a grey ring.

"I'll do the flowers myself, Annie, if you don't mind," said Susan as she thumbed through the telephone book for a french polisher. Annie felt like a naughty child.

Of course she still played with the children and enjoyed them. She baby-sat quite often but had to admit that Susan didn't *use* her, and she and Joe grudged her nothing.

"Why don't you go into town and get a new coat. Put it on the account. Get a camel . . . that's always nice . . . and maybe a tweed skirt. And for goodness' sake get some tights! How can you bear these things?" And Annie glanced out at the two limp stockings dangling on the line beside her corsets. They did look a bit pathetic. But that's what she'd always worn.

Susan wasn't lazy either. She swept like a whirlwind through the house three times a week with hoover and duster. Even did Annie's room.

"That little dog ornament on your dressing-table's cracked, Annie. You don't want to keep it do you? And I see you've a

182

pile of jumpers and shoes in the bottom of your wardrobe. Why don't we send them to the W.V.S."

Exposed. That was it, really. That's what she felt. Susan and Joe knew about everything she did, everywhere she went, everything she had. Annie considered as she walked across the field path to the stone bridge. There was nothing about her life now that was not open to Susan. No secrets, no private treats. She knew fine that Susan repeated all her faults and foolishnesses to Joe at night. She had heard them. Susan had her little ways too, of course, but Annie had no one to gossip with about those, get them off her chest. Anyway it wouldn't have been right ever to complain about the family to outsiders.

For all Annie's firm resolutions to be no trouble, it got more difficult, as she had known it would. And it would get worse yet, for already there were fleeting, terrifying lapses into confusion and tricks of memory. As the years went on she would be more of a care to them. She trembled and waited in dread of catching the word 'Home' or 'Hospital'. She wanted to be where she was, with Joe and Susan and the children. More and more she thought about her grandfather and her mother.

Annie sighed. She would just have to let things be with the next generation, and skip them, to make friends with her grandchildren ... find an interest to share with them. Alison was six now, skinny like Joe but with her mother's blonde hair. Annie tried the eyebright and the bluebells and the looking for tadpoles, but there was no magic in these for Alison. And it would have been a cheek to teach Joe's daughter to make scones. She took to sitting in her room or in the garden, as she was doing now, knitting and half-dozing, hearing the children play, but not special to either of them.

She woke with a start, as she felt a small body wriggling in between her legs and examining the half-finished cardigan.

"Going to teach me to do that, Gran? Knit, I mean." Annie ruffled the fair hair. A quick vision possessed her of rainbow wool and six-inch pins, dropped stitches and dolls' scarves ... maybe later of embroidery silks and traycloths. She would irk

Susan and Joe to the end of her days. That was for sure. But perhaps that was the way it had always been, one generation grating on the next. You could feel closer to the one you'd no responsibility for. Knitting wasn't much, but it was the best terms Annie could come to, for the present.